THE DARK TOMB SEEMED COLD AND EERIE—

The dry chill of the vault seeped through me. Eagerly, I sought the glimmer of moonlight that should have been there ahead of me, seeping in through the low, arched doorway. But there was only a densely smothering darkness beyond the pale circle of light cast by my flickering lantern.

As I spun about in panic, the chilling grate of metal scraping against metal assaulted my eardrums as someone crashed the thick bolt that sealed the vault's doors viciously into place. I pounded on the resisting metal, commanding whoever was there beyond the solidly riveted panels to release me. But it was no use. *I was alone, locked inside my father's tomb!*

WOMAN IN BLACK

by
Monica Heath

A SIGNET BOOK
NEW AMERICAN LIBRARY
TIMES MIRROR

SIGNET, SIGNET CLASSICS, MENTOR, PLUME AND MERIDIAN BOOKS
are published by The New American Library, Inc.,
1301 Avenue of the Americas, New York, New York 10019

FIRST PRINTING, SEPTEMBER, 1974

1 2 3 4 5 6 7 8 9

PRINTED IN THE UNITED STATES OF AMERICA

Chapter ONE

Strong hands tugged at me and I let out a low moan, gratefully sliding back into the gray haze that softened the searing pain in my temples. Vaguely, I heard the familiar creak of straining leather accompanied by the restless stamp of horses' hooves and I tried desperately to remember—to account for the thudding ache that set off bevies of blazing rockets inside my head.

The stage. Was I still in the rumbling Conestoga being rattled and pummeled about unmercifully as the driver whipped the splendid team of black horses over the rutted, mountain roads? Had I dozed off for a second, been overwhelmed by the terrifying dream that still reached out to claim me?

"Silly little minx, dashing out like that," a man's voice said from somewhere close by. It was low, vibrant, and gently soothing, and something behind its pleasant tones sounded almost like fondness.

My father? A childish eagerness flooded through me and I tried to speak.

"Thank God you're still alive," the man said.

Alive. I had a hazy vision of a girl's painted face breaking into a cynical smile. I forced open my burning eyelids. But instead of that faintly familiar, foxlike countenance, I looked up into piercing brown eyes staring earnestly down at me from beneath fiercely beetled brows.

"Miss McKay? Julie?" The darkly rugged features hovering over me were chillingly familiar.

I recoiled, closing my eyes against the gritting tears flooded behind my dust-caked lids. But not before I had glimpsed bearded faces looming around me, and peering anxiously out at me through a break in the crowd, a woman's shocked visage, the paleness of her indefinable features making them seem oddly detached, like the hovering face of a ghost.

Eagerly I escaped back into the gray cloud, caught up once more by the swaying motion of the coach that had seemed destined to go on forever.

There had been nothing but canyons for as far as the eye could see, their gray flanks scarred by mine dumps below shaft houses which jutted up from the barren terrain like alien growths on the seamed side of some great, sprawling beast.

And all around us, tier upon tier of jagged mountains rent the fragile paleness of a summer sky veiled with the first hint of fall even though August had not yet begun.

Then, suddenly, the creaking coach had crested the head of the winding canyon that curved upward in a long, sweeping gash from Carson City to the sprawling mining town that clung tenaciously to the soaring slopes of Sun Mountain.

Virginia City. I wasn't quite certain what I had expected to find. Surely not the nakedly exposed buildings that tumbled haphazardly down hillsides devoid of any softening vegetation save for the silvery-gray sage and rabbit brush that thrived in such lavish abundance. There were none of the stately old trees I had grown accustomed to in the South to cast their protective shadows over the high, board walks; no velvety-green gardens rioting behind the listing picket fences that hemmed dusty yards where a few molting chickens scratched.

My heart gave a queer little lurch as my gaze was drawn to a huge, boxlike structure looming in the distance, secured by thick, dark chains to the rugged rise above the town. The chains, which had been exploited by the press at the time the house had been built, were a novelty my father ordered from a local blacksmith who had forged the mammoth links by hand. Their purpose was to secure the towering mansion against the Washoe zephyrs that swept with erratic savagery across the naked mountain slopes during the spring and fall months.

A breeze fluttered the sparse, dusty leaves of the gaunt poplar and locust trees that surrounded the three-story dwelling, sending a flickering of sunlight and shadow through its pillared galleries. The effect was curiously deceptive, imbuing the big house with a nostalgic air of gentility.

It pained me to see how closely McKay Mansion resembled the house I had lived in for nearly all of my life in Savannah. Only the great moss-draped live oaks and the ravaged rice fields that spread endlessly over the canal-threaded islands of the Ogeechee River were missing. My father, whose family had long since lost what little property they had owned through an endless series of crop failures and other financial mishaps, had once envied my uncle Grant his wealth and position as one of Georgia's most successful planters. Seeing the mansion that loomed so incongruously above the dusty, gray mining town made me realize for the first time just how deep his resentment had been. Although Uncle Grant had rarely mentioned my father, Aunt Hillary had never allowed my mother to forget that she had married beneath her station when she'd chosen John McKay.

There were other mansions dominating the town—the lavishly impressive homes of the *nouveaux riches* Comstock kings. But none was perched half so high nor was half so grand as the house my father had built for the woman he'd married after my mother's death, when I was nine. No one had guessed then that John McKay's unquenchable lust for gold would one day make him one of the richest men on the lode, least of all Aunt Hillary, who had taken my mother and me in when my father boarded the steamer at Savannah to go to the California gold fields. I had been only four at the time, and I had not seen him since, although he had endeavored, for a time, to keep in touch with us through long, newsy letters he'd penned by firelight in the far-flung mining camps.

Then gradually his letters had grown shorter, finally ceasing altogether save for a few hastily scrawled lines at Christmas.

"It's no use singing psalms to a dead horse," Aunt Hillary acquired a habit of saying. "If only you'd had better sense than to marry someone like John McKay, Cindy. What kind of a life is this for you and Julie, forced to scrounge off of your sister's husband? I suppose I shall never come to understand what it was you saw in him."

My mother was confined to her bed by then, partly from the chronic condition that had plagued her all of her life, and partly, I suspected, from heartache and loneliness.

Aunt Hillary's fiery tirades against my father became more venomous than ever after my mother's death, during the war, and my father's subsequent marriage to a widow named Isabel Ritchie. My aunt wasted no time accusing them both when word of their marriage reached us.

"I don't doubt for an instant that he was involved with this . . . this *adventuress* who now claims to be his wife even before poor Cindy passed away," she had said vehemently. "I suppose this means that you shall be with us permanently, Julie. The creature has a flock of ragged offspring of her own, it seems. Thank heaven you're only a year younger than your cousin Melissa, and can make-do with her castoffs."

Yet no one had followed my father's abrupt rise to wealth and fame more avidly than did Aunt Hillary when at last he stumbled onto the riches that had eluded him for so long. No longer a child, I had come to resent Aunt Hillary's obsessive attitude, and had it not been for Uncle Grant, who found his own practical ways to rescue me when a storm seemed to threaten, I might have flown at her like an angry tigress, for all of my gentle breeding.

As it was, I had a quick mind, which prompted Uncle Grant to assign me, at an early age, the task of keeping the plantation record books, thus providing me with an avenue of escape. But best of all, I had my father's letters. I had found them after my mother died, tied with a faded lavender ribbon and tucked into a hidden niche at the back of her rosewood desk. I spent long hours alone in my room after that, quietly saturating my mind with those outmoded details of his life, even though his face had long since faded to a hazy blur in the depths of my troubled mind.

"Vulgar!" Aunt Hillary became fond of saying about the big house I gazed out at now with an unbridled curiosity.

According to the Eastern press, the mansion my father had built for Isabel Ritchie and the stepbrothers and stepsister I had never seen rivaled New York's finest. Said to be filled with priceless treasures gleaned from every corner of the globe, I had been far more fascinated than I had quite dared to show by the detailed newspaper accounts of the priceless porcelains, silk-embroidered screens, and carved teakwood furnishings which my stepmother ordered on whim during her trips abroad.

One reporter had taken particular note of a large figurine made of solid silver taken from the McKay-Ritchie Mine and, as I continued to stare out through the coach window at the huge house, I tried to comprehend my father's fabulous wealth, even though it still pained me to realize that I might never have known of his good fortune had it not been for the excitement it had generated among the Eastern brokers.

Now that I was here, it mattered very little to me that the McKay name had gradually lost its magic claim to the public's interest as the journalists and reporters turned their attention to the stock devilment that became synonymous with the Comstock, following those first, rich strikes. The *Savannah Herald* had given only slight mention to the McKay-Ritchie Mine during the past few years, and virtually no mention at all of my father.

Had it not been for the letter I'd found hidden beneath the velvet lining of my cousin Melissa's jewelry casket, I might never have known that my father still thought of me as his beloved daughter, in spite of everything.

Chapter TWO

The letter. I stirred and the same voice that had spoken before said, "Just lie quietly. I'm taking you to Dr. Quinn to make certain nothing's broken. It's only a little way now. I'll try not to hurt you any more than I have to."

For a second or two I imagined that I was still rollicking along in the lumbering stagecoach, caught up tenaciously in the web of that same terrifying dream. Then it came to me that I was awake and that the man who had spoken to me was carrying me in his arms. I opened my eyes to late-afternoon sunlight streaming through a shimmering cloud of dust motes onto his tanned face.

"Father?" I whispered.

Then I realized that the face above me was far too young to belong to my father.

"You *can't* be John McKay," I said accusingly.

"Never mind that now." Something flickered behind his dark features, his eyes gleaming with golden lights like the piercing stare of a hawk.

"The letter," I murmured again, fumbling for my reticule.

The frayed cord, which matched the braid on my green bombazine travel gown, was no longer wound tightly around my wrist.

A wave of panic surged through me.

"Who are you?" I forced out the frightened words between parched lips, vaguely aware that I had seen the man before, peering out at me from some dimly shadowed place.

Had he been a part of the dream? I tried to remember. But before I could collect my numbed thoughts, one of the bearded miners jostled against us, sending a dizzying jag of pain through my aching head.

Even as I heard his softly muttered curse, the gray haze closed around me and I slipped quietly back into oblivion.

I had found the last of my father's letters purely by chance and, as the big red-and-gold painted coach rolled noisily down the final grade toward the town, my nervous fingers pinched the frayed cloth of my reticule to make certain it was still there, tucked safely inside. I had slept with the string of the small bag twined tightly around my wrist throughout the long journey by train and coach, haunted by an unreasonable fear that someone, guessing how dear it was to me, might try to take it from me, as Cousin Melissa had done.

The letter might still have been hidden at the bottom of Melissa's jewelry casket had it not been for the ivory-satin ball gown my cousin had given me which required her butter-amber beads to hide the small, ugly spill on its bodice. When I asked my cousin's permission to wear the beads, she promptly refused me. It was Aunt Hillary who had insisted that Melissa learn to share her belongings more generously.

"Find them for yourself, then," Melissa had snapped at me that fateful day, her narrow mouth drooping petulantly to reveal her small, sharp teeth.

The thin pages of the letter crackled softly beneath the chest's torn lining as I searched through its tangled contents, feeling a peculiar excitement that stifled any qualms I might have had as I hastily ripped the frayed velvet loose from its carved frame. Later, I told myself that I had known what I would find even before I glimpsed the familiar handwriting on the torn envelope.

The letter was dated June 11, 1867, which meant that Melissa had kept it hidden from me for nearly a year.

My dear daughter, began the flowing script that had already begun to fade. *I suppose by now you must think your old father has forgotten all about his little girl. But nothing could be farther from the truth, dear Julie. You dwell forever in my heart and my thoughts and it is for this very reason that I have taken my pen in hand to send you these few lines.*

No doubt you have learned by now that I came into my own good fortune shortly after I married Isabel Ritchie, who is now Mrs. McKay and your stepmother, dear girl, even though the two of you have never met. Your aunt Hillary made it quite clear to me by post, following your dear mother's passing, that she considered me a scoundrel and had no further desire to communicate with yours truly.

But I assure you, dear daughter, that I intended no insult to either you or your dear, departed mother's memory when I wed Isabel Ritchie and became as a father to her four homeless waifs. Be assured that, at the time, we were both as ships adrift and badly in need of an anchor.

To prove my continuing loyalty, I am leaving you a legacy in the hope that you will remember me with kindness. I have yet to consult my agents concerning this important matter. But please believe me when I tell you that on the morrow, all necessary details shall be dutifully dispatched. I have this same night composed and drafted a signed paper setting forth my wishes concerning you and it waits only to be witnessed and recorded by the proper authorities to be rendered indisputable.

The letter was signed *John McKay.*

Tears welled behind my eyelids as I recalled its contents, dimming my view of the mansion that intimidated me even as I felt drawn by a profound curiosity to it and the people who lived there. I tried again, as I had done so often during these past weeks, to imagine why Melissa, who had obviously read the letter before hiding it away, had wanted to keep the good news of my heritage from me. Knowing how desperately I would seize upon any word from my father after such a long silence, had she tucked the letter away, intending to use it as an instrument of coercion at some future date and then promptly forgotten about it?

I had inadvertently discovered far more than Melissa had intended for me to know concerning her illicit dallyings with Roger Beauchamp, a young man who had neither family nor breeding and whom both Aunt Hillary and Uncle Grant disapproved of wholeheartedly. Under the circumstances, I could only assume that Melissa had feared the consequences of the forbidden knowledge I had gleaned when I came upon the two of them wrapped shamelessly in each other's arms late one night when I slipped out for a breath of air beneath the moss-studded live oaks that lent dignity to the white-columned plantation house. How else could I explain my cousin's treachery? Being the kind of person she was, Melissa could not have known that it wasn't in me to betray her deceitful actions, and so the letter had stayed hidden and no doubt forgotten until the day I had gone to her room to search for the amber beads she'd so grudgingly lent me.

It had been dismayingly easy, after the letter came into my possession, to convince Aunt Hillary and Uncle Grant that my father was eager for me to join him in Virginia City. I had been fully aware at the time that such was not actually the case.

But because I had found myself wanting so badly to escape the plantation where I would always be regarded as a poor relative, I had succeeded in convincing myself that it had been my father's real intention for me to read between the lines. The fact that he had arranged to leave me a legacy became superfluous to the message I imagined was there.

Once again, Uncle Grant came to my rescue, quickly dispelling any trepidations Aunt Hillary may have had over seeing me set off on such an arduous journey, unescorted, when he stated in his most authoritarian voice that he would personally see to it that the travel-company agents kept a safe watch over me.

He could not have said more plainly that he was glad to be rid of me.

The thought had crossed my mind, when I saw how eager Uncle Grant was to let me go, that it would be advantageous to him in more ways than one to let me go with no great fuss. Stripped of his wealth when Sherman took Savannah during the war to present it to Lincoln as a Christmas gift, Uncle Grant deemed it doubly important for Melissa to wed a man with promising connections. My mirror had told me often enough that I was the one who'd had the good fortune to inherit my mother's and Aunt Hillary's delicate-seeming, auburn-haired beauty, an appraisal I had seen reflected often enough in the eyes of the local gallants who came to call. While poor Melissa, who took after Uncle Grant's side of the family with her stubborn jawline and sharply jutting nose, had scarcely any looks at all.

Nevertheless, I shuddered to think what Uncle Grant, who had a damnable temper, might have done had he learned of Melissa's nighttime dalliances with Roger and I felt suddenly glad that I was no longer a part of their lives.

Concentrating my attention on the house chained above the town, I noted that it had a hip roof studded with dormers, their leaded panes shimmering darkly beneath ornately fluted pediments. A square cupola thrust up from the center of the flat roof, partially hidden behind a balustraded rail, and as the coach rattled past the piles of earth and ore that spilled haphazardly down the mountain's honeycombed slopes, I had the sudden, uncomfortable feeling that someone watched secretly from behind the dome's arched windows. Was it one of the Steps, as I had come to think of my stepbrothers and stepsister, or perhaps my stepmother, Isabel, who had gone there to watch for my arrival?

It occurred to me that my father had failed to tell me anything about his wife and family in his letter. I attempted to picture them in my mind's eye, and as the thundering coach plunged headlong into town I tried not to think that my father was as much a stranger to me as they.

The uneasy thought was driven from my mind by a barrage of strange sounds that assaulted my ears from every side, arousing my fellow passenger, a flamboyant girl not much older than myself who for the past half-hour had been dozing against the stiff leather cushions opposite me.

"Kinda naked and raw, ain't it, honey." The girl, who had boarded the stage at Placerville, rubbed sleep from heavily painted eyelids. "But it's alive and that's more than can be said for a lot of places. There's nothing worse than a wore-out mining camp, take my word for it, deary."

"I'd scarcely call Virginia City a camp," I said uncertainly above the shrill, hissing puff of a steam engine that mingled with the pounding roar of the stamp mills farther down the slope.

From farther away came the thunderous boom of subterranean blasts, shaking the very earth beneath the coach's wheels.

Nearer at hand, carpenters ripped and sawed and hammered, sending up their own raucous volley that all but drowned the cracked voice of a fruit vendor peddling his wares from a rickety cart. I could not entirely ignore the colorful curses of the teamsters who bellowed at strings of rawboned mules hitched to the laden ore wagons that crept at a snail's pace through the very heart of the city.

Incongruously, a six-story brick hotel thrust up behind the crawling wagons and I glimpsed women, clad in the most stylish Eastern fashions, mingling with the flannel-shirted miners who thronged the busy street.

"I guess maybe you're right about this not being a camp anymore, honey," the girl seated across from me conceded. "I heard it's the biggest town between St. Louis and San

Francisco. But being a born skeptic, I had to come see it for myself. Might be if I stay around long enough I'll end up with the sealskin cape I promised myself way last Christmas. I've heard it said there's still plenty of big spenders on the lode, men like Greg Gallagher and Royce Ritchie, although they say Gallagher's a queer sort of duck. But I reckon I've handled worse."

Royce Ritchie. Was it possible she was referring to a member of my father's family? I had no idea how old the Steps were. Waifs, my father had called them in his letter. But it had been nearly ten years since he had first become a father to Isabel Ritchie's brood.

I wanted to ask the girl about Royce Ritchie. But, like the town that spilled nakedly down the barren slopes of Sun Mountain, I found her a trifle bewildering. I could only guess that she was somewhere near my own age, which was only a few weeks short of twenty, for there was a sophisticated gloss about her that had very little to do with age, that seemed to have molded her pert features into a brittle, foxlike mask which appeared to crack whenever she flashed me one of her cynical little smiles. The effect was one of reckless bravado tempered by an infinite wisdom that made me feel suddenly gauche.

For a faltering instant, I wished I was back home in Savannah.

Then, as the coach came to a screeching halt in front of the Wells Fargo Company office, the driver leaping adroitly down from his perch to help me out onto the dusty street, an excited eagerness took hold of me and I thought: *This is my home, now, here in this lively town with my father.*

Haughtily ignoring the shyly speculative glances cast my way by several of the bearded men who passed through the swinging doors of a place called The Red Dog, I picked up my travel-worn skirts and stepped gingerly onto the high-curbed walk. My whole body grew taut with that same urgent sense of eagerness as I paused briefly to scan the churning crowd for some sign of my father, turning about in confusion when I failed to find his dimly remembered features among the sea of faces.

Sudden, shrill laughter rose above the rumble of male

voices that spilled out of the nearby saloon and I turned to see the girl who had been on the stage step boldly inside, the plumes on her smart little hat bobbing bravely. Feeling more inexperienced than ever in my prim, coal-scuttle bonnet—one of Melissa's castoffs—I continued to scan the busy street, a chilling apprehension stealing over me.

Where *was* my father? Why had he failed to meet me? What if he didn't come at all? Would I then dare to approach the mansion alone, not knowing how the others who lived there felt about me? My anxiety grew as I continued to ponder the dismaying barrage of questions that flooded my mind and it occurred to me for the first time that my father might never have received the letter I had posted weeks before, in Savannah, to let him know I was coming. There had been no reply from him, nor had there been a response to the wire I had sent him from Sacramento before embarking on the final leg of my journey.

Now I realized that I had taken it for granted that he would meet me, as eagerly enthusiastic about renewing our familial bond as I was. But apparently such was not the case, for no vaguely familiar figure disengaged itself from the restless bands of men that continued to flow in and out through the swinging doors of The Red Dog. Nor was there anyone about who even remotely resembled him as I'd come to picture him in my mind's eye.

Fiddle-footed. Unreliable. Aunt Hillary's bitter accusations returned to haunt me. I looked longingly up at the mansion that stood at the top of one of the steeply winding cross streets. There was no hint of life behind its glowering facade, only those darkly leaded panes glaring coldly down at me.

I turned quickly away.

An inordinate amount of activity seethed around me, seeming in itself to be Virginia City's *raison d'être* and, in spite of the misgivings I was beginning to feel, I felt infected by it, watching in stunned fascination when a bevy of blond women dressed in matching costumes brushed past my piled luggage, their voluptuous forms barely controlled by their corset strings.

A dapper little man with a short upper lip and round,

greedy eyes followed in their giggling wake, recklessly dispensing a handful of fliers. He slipped a handbill from the thick sheaf and thrust it into my gloved fingers.

"The Red Stocking Blondes," he informed me unnecessarily. "Best show in town. Piper's Opera House tonight at eight."

His daring, black eyes lingered overlong on my face, causing a warm glow to rise beneath the sheltering scoop of my bonnet, and I found myself thinking, when he had turned away from me with a pleased little chuckle, that the fox-faced girl on the stage had been right: the town was alive—more than a little bit scandalous for all of its civilized pretentions.

My growing fascination with the thriving city was dimmed only by my father's continuing absence. I tried to tell myself then that he had been detained for some pressing reason. But it was no use. For if that were the case, he would surely have sent one of the Steps to fetch me.

Looking at my situation in the cold light of logic, there seemed nothing left for me to do but hire a rig to drive me and my trunks up the hill to the hovering mansion. After asking the travel agent to keep a watch on my baggage, I struck off determinedly in the direction of a barn-like structure on the far side of the street; above its door a sign read: Hansen's Livery. The line of ore wagons continued to move slowly through the center of town, blocking my progress, and I paused on the corner to wait for them to pass. Chunks of gray ore spilled out from beneath their tailgates, disappearing into the clouds of pale dust that rose up from their cumbersome wheels.

Suddenly a gentle breeze stirred past me, wafting away the thick cloud to reveal the name stenciled on their green-painted sideboards: *McKay-Ritchie Mining Company.* In that same instant, I became aware of a tall man watching me from the far side of the street. His face appeared to be darkly weathered, blending into the shadows beneath a low-hanging gallery.

It was his eyes that gave him away. Even in that muted light they seemed to be fire-bright, gazing out at me with an intensity that sent an involuntary shudder through my travel-weary body.

Chapter THREE

I wasn't dreaming after all. I pushed back the gray haze, forcing open my eyes. The man who cradled my aching body in arms folded around me like steel bands was the same man who had watched me earlier from the shadows beneath the gallery.

He glanced down and saw me looking up at him.

"You're safe now," he said softly.

"What do you want with me?" I whispered weakly. "Why . . . ?" The thought spun itself out silently against the throbbing backdrop of my mind: *Why did you try to kill me?*

It was all coming back to me: a tall form lounging with deceptive grace beneath the balustraded gallery; dark eyes snapping like live coals, their determined gaze never wavering from my face.

I had scurried off in an effort to escape that burning stare, all but crashing into a strutting Indian. Stifling a little scream, I looked up into sloe-black eyes set close beside a hooked nose, a sense of unreality seizing me. The Indian was clad, unbelievably, in a bobtailed coat covered with buttons. Bits and pieces of brass dangled from his greasy tresses, more of the gleaming pieces studding the plug hat that rode jauntily on his head. After giving me a gutteral grunt, he loped away down the street.

The Mad Hatter. I had read the recent sensational book by Charles Dodgson, penned for the daughter of a friend under the pseudonym of Lewis Carroll, and even though it had been publicized originally as a book for children, its irony and absurdity had amused me at the time.

Now, suddenly, I felt as if, like Alice, I had been plunged headlong into some dim netherworld where the grotesque had become the commonplace. Picking up my bedraggled skirts, I waited for an opening to appear between the creeping ore wagons, pushing aside the terrifying fact that I had no money for my return fare to Savannah, nor any real assurance that my father really wanted me.

Stealing a desperate glance across my shoulder, I saw, with a wild surge of relief, that the man who had watched me from the shadows beneath the gallery was no longer there. His presence had dismayed me more than I had realized, for almost at once my outlook brightened and I was able then to smile at the swaggering Indian who was still visible a short distance down the square.

Moments later, the break I sought appeared between the lumbering freighters and I dashed headlong into the street, my flying feet churning up small clouds of dust that rose to choke me.

There was a sudden, sharp, cracking noise and someone shouted a warning. Without slowing my pace, I turned to see the broadly glistening chests of a team of handsome bays bearing down on me, their nostrils flaring as the man standing in the rig behind them flicked an evil-looking whip across their flanks.

Frantically I flung myself forward in an effort to escape their flashing hooves. But I was too late. The plunging beasts were onto me before I could bound to safety on the high-curbed walk, a powerful shoulder grazing past me to send me flying headlong into the smothering dust.

Rough boards rose to meet me, sending a sickening thud through my numbed brain, and I felt myself sinking slowly into a strangling gray oblivion.

But not before I had recognized the man who stood in the gleaming carriage behind the charging horses, his lean body braced stiffly against the straining reins. My last impression as I slid quietly into that smothering gray cloud was of his blazing eyes glaring triumphantly down at me, and I found myself wondering almost idly why he had wanted to destroy me.

Now I said wonderingly, "I'm still alive."

"Through no fault of your own," he said, jolting me painfully up a dimly lighted stair.

His words seemed to challenge me and I said, aware of

a betraying quaver in my voice, "May I remind you that you are the one who attempted to run me down, Mr.—" My voice trailed off feebly as I realized that I was at his mercy.

"Gallagher. Greg Gallagher," he said, his tone of voice implying that he took for granted that he would be recognized.

It seemed oddly ironic that I should have heard his name mentioned only a short while before, and I tried to recall what the girl on the stage had said about him. *A big spender. An odd sort of duck.* He was all of that, I conceded. But there had been nothing in her rambling revelations to indicate *who* he was or why he might want to harm me.

I said, "I seem to have regained my senses, sir. You may put me down now, if you please."

"And if I don't please?"

"I shall report you to my father."

Surprisingly, he obeyed me then, setting me down abruptly before a darkly varnished door that had the name *Dr. Thomas Quinn* stenciled across it in gold letters.

"Dr. Quinn is a friend of mine," he said, reaching to turn the knob.

"I'm certain a man like you must have a great many friends," I retorted, thinking again of the fox-faced girl on the stage.

"I had hoped I might have the privilege of counting you among them, Miss McKay. Julie," he added softly, darting out a steadying arm when I found myself beginning to totter.

My abortive effort to resume some semblance of composure had consumed all of my strength and I yielded gratefully when he swooped to lift me, going with me to one of the heavy, oak chairs that lined a darkly papered waiting room.

Julie. He had called me Julie before. But how had he known who I was? A dizzying wave of confusion swept over me and I sat with closed eyes, trying desperately to put the pieces together.

It occurred to me that perhaps my father had sent him to meet me. That could account for his knowing my name. But why had he tried to kill me?

I opened my eyes. "Do you know my father?" I asked hopefully. "Did he send you to meet my stage?"

He regarded me gravely. "No one sent me," he said. "Surely you know. . . ." He broke off with a weary shake of his head.

Something in his voice alerted me.

"Know what?" I demanded.

"That I now own the mine."

"The mine?" My stunned thoughts fumbled in an effort to grasp his meaning.

"The McKay-Ritchie."

I stared disbelievingly into his dark face. "But there must be some mistake. Surely my father would have said something when he wrote to me. Especially since I am to share in his estate when he's gone."

I knew at once that I had been foolish to reveal so much. But Greg Gallagher's claim that he owned the McKay-Ritchie Mine had caused me to throw caution to the winds. Now I saw that it would be equally foolish for me to try to dissemble. Already, an avid curiosity burned behind his eyes.

To my immense relief, a door opened on the far side of the room and a slight, blond man appeared. When he saw Greg, he asked with an odd urgency, "Has something happened? Is it—"

Greg cut him off sharply. "It's not what you think, Tom. There's been an accident on the street. This young lady darted out in front of my rig and was struck down."

The blond man seemed to see me for the first time.

Hurrying toward me, he thrust out his hand. "I'm Dr. Quinn. If you'll just come with me, Miss. . . ." His blue eyes gleamed curiously behind gold-rimmed spectacles.

"Miss McKay," I said.

There was no mistaking the sudden reflex that tightened the slender fingers grasping my wrist. He glanced quickly past me at Greg, his puzzled look demanding an explanation.

"Miss McKay arrived on the afternoon stage," Greg said.

"My father was supposed to meet me," I told Dr. Quinn. "I can't imagine what's kept him. Unless there's been trouble at the mine." I shot Greg Gallagher a challenging look, only to find him watching me in that queer, bright way he had.

"Tom will look after you," he said. "When he's finished, I'll drive you to the mansion."

There seemed to be nothing for me to do then but to allow myself to be led away and pummeled by Dr. Quinn, who pronounced me fit save for a minor concussion and an odd assortment of scrapes and bruises. I caught a distinct smell of whiskey on his breath when he leaned over me to dress the wound on my temple. Despite the smell of spirits clinging to him, his hands were steady and surprisingly gentle. They seemed to hold some magic power to soothe away my trepidations and I found myself liking him, and not just because he had a kindly manner that appealed to me, but because I imagined I saw some deeply abiding sorrow behind his solemn face, which was tempered generously with compassion.

"I want you to rest for a few days," he told me when he had finished with the plaster. "There will be some pain for a while, I'm afraid. But a little laudanum should take care of it."

He went to a large cabinet that held rows of neatly labeled apothecary bottles carefully arranged behind its leaded doors. It was then, as I watched him pour a few drops of the gray liquid into a glass vial, that I remembered my reticule, which contained all of the money I owned in the world, tucked into the torn envelope with my father's letter.

Taking the bottle Dr. Quinn handed me, I hurried into the waiting room, where I found Greg Gallagher waiting impatiently before a tall window that looked down on the teeming street. He turned at the sound of my footsteps, the moody look on his face giving way to a grudging smile.

"I trust Tom found you still all of a piece," he said.

"I'll be perfectly fine in no time," I said. "Except that I seem to have misplaced my bag. It must have fallen into the street when I . . . when I fell," I added hurriedly, wanting suddenly to believe that my little tragedy had been an accident after all. "I wonder if you might be so kind as to—"

He silenced me with an impatient gesture. Dipping slim fingers into his jacket pocket, he brought out my reticule.

"Is this what you're so concerned about?" He thrust the small pouch, which was soggy with street dust, into my eager hands. "It seems to be a bit the worse for wear, I'm afraid. But we can remedy that soon enough. I feel I owe it to you, Miss McKay . . . Julie, to furnish you with a new gown and bag. It's the least I can do, under the circumstances. At your convenience, of course. I have a . . . friend who knows of a good dressmaker."

Friend. Again I thought of the fox-faced girl who had been on the stage, an unfamiliar feeling charging through me.

"No thank you, Mr. Gallagher," I said, aware of a certain coldness in my voice. "These will do me nicely."

The return of my reticule had restored my confidence. Twining the familiar drawstring around my wrist, I reached to tie my bonnet firmly in place beneath a chin still smarting where a chunk of ore hidden in the street dust had grazed away a small patch of skin.

"You'd best take her home now, Greg," Dr. Quinn said.

Home. I recalled how dismal the mansion had looked, its glaring windows seeming to hide some darkly threatening evil. But it was my father's house and there was nowhere else for me to go.

Stiffening my spine, I turned to give Thomas Quinn a grateful little smile. "If you would be so kind as to bill my father," I said.

There was a sudden, awkward silence.

Then Greg said, taking a firm grip on my arm, "That's something else I owe you, Julie. The right to cover Tom's fee."

"But you don't owe me a thing," I retorted.

"Greg?" Dr. Quinn's voice sounded slightly querulous.

"I'll attend to it in due time, Tom," Greg said, steering me quickly out onto the landing.

But not before I had caught the subtle undercurrent of concern that flashed between them. I recalled then that there had been alarm in Thomas Quinn's voice when he had opened the door of his inner office to find Greg Gallagher standing in his waiting room. It was only after Greg had directed the doctor's attention to my inconspicuous presence that his anxiety had left him, giving way to a peculiar calm.

Chapter FOUR

It took Greg a surprisingly short while to load my trunks into his carriage.

"It's way and by far the most impressive house in town," I said when we had started up the hill toward the mansion.

He flashed me a look, something that might have been disdain flooding behind his handsome features, before he turned his attention back to the horses, flicking out at them with the long whip to send them flying at a reckless pace up the treacherous slope.

"You evaded me when I asked if you knew my father." In an attempt to appear casual, I looked out at the buildings flying past us.

"I knew him," he said shortly.

"I take it something happened to dim your opinion of him," I said. "Or perhaps his opinion of you?"

"I don't feel it's my place to try to explain things." His voice was grim.

"Naturally I'm curious. It's been such a long while since I last saw him. I can't help wondering what he's like now."

I was playing frankly on his sympathies. But it did me no good. He remained sternly uncommunicative.

I tried again. "I suppose you know that he was among the first men to come West. 'To see the elephant,' they called it then. He boarded a steamer at Savannah that took him to Chagres, where he joined with four other passengers to contract a canoe which carried them up the river to Cruces during their crossing of the Isthmus."

"If you are trying to tell me he deserved to be rich if any man did, I agree."

"I'm still wondering why you claim to own the McKay-Ritchie Mine," I said.

"I should think that would be obvious."

"But I don't understand your motives."

"I made that claim because I *am* the owner. Nothing could be plainer than that. They sold out to me after the vein went dry," he continued, and I could only stare disbelievingly at him.

"My father and Isabel?" I finally asked.

"Isabel and the others," he said obscurely.

"Then you and my father are partners? But I should think you'd have changed the name of the mine to the McKay-Gallagher if that were truly the case."

"The name of a mine is never changed." He curled the whip furiously over the horses' glistening flanks. "There are certain legal reasons for retaining the original name of a strike."

"Isabel brought my father luck," I said. "I suppose that's why he named the mine for her and her children by her first husband."

"Your father and Isabel owned adjoining claims." His voice was cynical.

"Are you suggesting that they married for that reason?"

"It's a possibility," he said in that same skeptical voice.

I stared ahead at the mansion, a cool breeze soothing my tired flesh. The last lingering rays of a setting sun gilded its pristine galleries, shimmering like blood on the shadowy panes of the tall windows. For the first time I noticed the weathered stones of a cemetery peering out of the scrub that carpeted the slope beyond the house. A large monument dominated the dismal assortment of gray headstones. Erected in the form of a Grecian temple, it sheltered the dimly visible gates of a mausoleum built into the hillside. For no discernible reason, a small shudder jarred through me, setting off an aching throb in my temple. Feeling suddenly faint, I slipped the strings of my reticule from my wrist and fumbled inside for the smelling salts Aunt Hillary had insisted on tucking in at the last minute.

Then I discovered that my father's letter was missing. Tugging frantically at the frayed cord, I sorted through the bag's contents. But it was no use. The precious missive was gone.

I stole a look at Greg Gallagher's hawklike profile. He seemed lost in his own thoughts, unaware of my sudden distress. Or was he even more devious than I had already begun to suspect?

The street turned to wind toward the mountain's summit, past the Miners' Union and Piper's Opera House. I stared gloomily ahead, trying to think of what to do, noticing vaguely that one of the sleek, reddish horses hitched to the carriage had a streak of clotted blood across its rump. I was ready to add cruelty to the list of grievances I was rapidly compiling against Greg Gallagher until I realized how expertly he snapped the evil-seeming whip over the animals' flanks, never allowing it to quite touch their gleaming hides.

Recalling the loud, snapping sound I had heard just before I'd been struck down by one of the plunging beasts, I thought: He can be cruel when it suits his purpose. The sudden, cracking noise had reverberated like gunfire. It must have been then that he'd lacerated the poor beast's flesh. I found the thought highly distasteful, and turned my attention away from the wounded animal to the houses terraced above us.

The row of residences stairstepped against the rugged slope became increasingly impressive as we climbed toward the mansion that seemed suddenly to strain at its ugly black chains to loom starkly over us. Apprehension tugged chillingly at me. What if they turned me away? What if my father didn't want me after all? What if I had read far more into his letter than he had intended?

It wouldn't bear thinking about and I turned to Greg to ask about a house that had caught my eye. Located next to the mansion, it rivaled my father's house for size and grandeur, a polygonal cupola perched above its sharply pitched roof. Stone steps set like a stile against a high retaining wall of natural field stone led up to a barred gate hinged in a viciously spiked fence.

"It belongs to me," Greg said of the house that had English slide shutters obscuring its tall bay windows.

I knew well enough that the purpose of the shutters was to protect the rich furnishings inside from the damaging sunlight. Nevertheless, a shudder swept over me at the sight of those darkened windows that lent an effect of mystery to a house that might have otherwise been attractive.

"I can't imagine you living there," I said, assuming that the house was closed since it appeared to be much too large for a man living alone.

"As a matter of fact, I do live there." He gave me a casual smile.

"Alone?" I blurted curiously.

He glanced suspiciously at me. As if, like his house, he had some dark secret to hide.

"Except for my housekeeper," he said then.

We continued on in silence, the horses straining against the sharp rise. The cemetery on the slopes above the mansion had become plainly visible, the rows of stones marching in stark relief across the stark dips and gullies. I glimpsed marble benches inside the Grecian temple which was joined to a large outcropping of natural stone so that it seemed to grow out of the face of the mountain.

I felt Greg watching me.

"Your father is there," he said gently when I turned to face him.

I stared at him uncomprehendingly.

"He died nearly a year ago," he said.

"How?" I whispered.

"He was murdered," Greg said quietly.

Murdered. The carriage seemed to tilt precariously.

"But he *can't* be dead," I whispered senselessly when it had righted itself, the mountain swimming once again into its proper perspective beyond a coach house that had appeared behind the mansion, set into the mountainside like the marble tomb.

"I can't imagine why you weren't told," he said.

I stared up helplessly at the mansion's tightly shuttered windows. There was still no sign of life behind the blankly gleaming panes and a dizzying panic swooped over me. What if there was no one there? What if Isabel and the

Steps were off somewhere on one of their buying jaunts? Where would I go then? What would I do? I had no money. The few dollars I'd had left after my journey had been with the missing letter.

A curving drive led around the house to a side door. Reining the horses to a halt, Greg leaped out to help me down. I stepped onto a flagstone walk set unbelievably between tiny patches of lawn that had been burned to a pale coppery shade by the summer sun. The smell of sage was all around me. Gulping the pungent air to clear my head, I lifted my skirts and went bravely to the door.

Glancing back briefly, I saw Greg waiting almost warily beside the carriage and I knew instinctively that he wasn't welcome in my father's house.

The woman who answered my nervous rap was elderly, at least as old as my father would have been, had he still been alive.

"I'd like to see Mrs. John McKay, please," I said, mistaking her at first for a maid.

Then, as she inched open the door and I saw her face more clearly, I realized that she must be my stepmother, Isabel.

A diamond brooch glittered on the bosom of her black crepe dress below features that were sharply regal, set as they were between thick silvery wings of hair. Her lips suggested a courteous smile, belying the frankly curious look that brightened eyes which were a peculiar shade of green.

"I'm Mrs. McKay," she said after a slight hesitation.

Relief washed through me and I said breathlessly as dizzyness threatened to overtake me once again, "I'm Julie. I wrote my father to let him know I was coming."

The woman stared suspiciously at me. "If you are referring to my husband, he passed away some months ago, I regret to say."

Now that the letter was no longer in my possession, there seemed to be no way I could prove my identity.

"Surely he spoke of me," I said a little desperately.

But she was no longer paying any attention to me. Her gaze had strayed to the tall man who lounged, with what now appeared to be a defiant insolence, against the carriage braked at the end of the walk.

"Sam!" Isabel called without taking her eyes off of him.

A small, elderly Chinese scurried softly out from the shadows behind her. She gestured briefly toward the waiting carriage where my baggage was clearly visible, stacked neatly in the boot.

"Please bring Miss McKay's trunks inside," she ordered.

Imperturbable, the small, yellow man backed away with a deep bow and hurried off, his shuffling feet moving soundlessly across the worn stones.

Glancing at Greg, I saw a corner of his mouth lift in a triumphant smile when Isabel turned haughtily away, the clash of their wills charging the air around me with a seething hostility.

"That man murdered my husband," Isabel snapped at me when Greg had gone.

I gave her a stunned stare.

"I find it a little strange that he should be the one to bring you here," she said.

"But how could I possibly have known?" I protested. "If I had—" I broke off, not certain what I would have done. "After all, John McKay was my father," I added helplessly.

"That remains to be seen," Isabel said.

Chapter FIVE

The room Isabel took me to overlooked Greg Gallagher's house and I found myself staring out unbidden through the thinly laced leaves of the poplar and locust trees at its upper stories which seemed more darkly shuttered than ever. It was as if, somehow, both the house and its occupants sensed that I looked out curiously from behind the Belgian lace curtains and had drawn more tightly in upon themselves out of some onerously shared instinct that prompted them to conceal whatever forbidden secrets were sheltered by those blackly glaring panes.

I turned toward Isabel, who stood just inside the doorway, watching me out of shrewd eyes that mirrored a sharp suspicion.

"It would never have done for me to have had this out with you in Greg Gallagher's presence," she said when Sam, who had followed us up the stairs with my portmanteau, had bowed out, on subservient feet, of the lavishly furnished room. "It would have been an unforgivable breach of etiquette and I have my position in this town to consider. That's the only reason I've seen fit to bring you into my house, Miss . . . whatever your rightful name happens to be," she added, fixing me with her piercing stare. "I sensed that you came here prepared to argue your cause and, as you shall discover for yourself, I'm not an unkind woman, nor unfair in my judgments of others. Obviously, you are weary from your journey. We will discuss your claim later, after you've had a suitable chance to rest and refresh yourself."

"There is no need for disagreement," I said, aware that here was a woman who took her role as one of the town's leading ladies far more seriously than I might have guessed was possible, basing my judgment on the kind of man my father had been. He had not been one to put on airs, in spite of his resentment of Uncle Grant's wealth and prestige. His envy, if it could have been called that, had grown out of his dislike of Aunt Hillary, who had seized every available opportunity to belittle him in my own and my mother's presence, even before he had decided to leave us behind to seek his fortune in the California gold fields.

"Surely you don't expect me to admit you as a member of my household without first making certain who you are?" Isabel said regally. "If it turns out that you are a respectable young woman who is momentarily down on her luck, I'm certain something can be arranged. I'm a civic-minded woman, as well I should be."

Although Isabel's words weren't openly boastful, I saw more than a hint of arrogance in her that would not be daunted by her drab though fashionable widow's weeds. Here was a woman, I quickly decided, who looked upon herself as a paragon of social virtue, knowledgeable of the finer amenities, but not above assisting those who might be less fortunate than herself, in her role as one of the boisterous town's wealthier benefactresses.

The Eastern press had made frequent mention of the balls and other frivolities that were held in an effort to raise funds for the destitute families of miners who had died in cave-ins or had been struck down by the dreaded lung fever that apparently killed a goodly number of them in their prime.

"But I've told you who I am," I protested in the wake of what was, admittedly, a hasty effort to assess her character. "You must believe me. How could I possibly have known of the existence of someone named Julie McKay if I were not, in fact, she. Surely you are aware that my father had been married before and that there was a daughter from that first marriage. It was all quite proper, I assure you. My mother, who had been an invalid for some time, died rather suddenly. He can't have failed to tell you that. Or about me," I added imploringly.

"My husband was never given to deceit," Isabel admitted. "He informed me that there had been a wife and child in the States, of course. It became common knowledge, after we became rich. Anyone could have read about it in the papers. The reporters were fond of composing vignettes around every facet of our lives, past and present. Their careless revelations came to be a nuisance in time, as I've already explained to you. They served to draw undesirables to us—drifters and other ill-assorted types bent on exploitation."

There was no mistaking her inference: that I might well be yet another member of that ill-assorted horde that had descended on the Comstock like hungry locusts in the wake of the first fabulous discoveries, intent on taking, by every manner of ill-conceived means, a share of the incredible wealth that spilled out of the mines.

"But I am that child my father left behind in the States," I said firmly, desperation momentarily dimming the fiercely thudding pain in my temple that lent a strange sense of unreality to my predicament. I had an overwhelming impulse to pinch myself to make certain that I had not dozed off on the thundering stage and become involved in some shattering nightmare that proved to be dismayingly real. Stifling the childish urge, I went on in that same firm but frantic voice, "How can you possibly doubt me? I should never have known where to come, had I not had some recent contact with my father."

"My husband has been dead for more than a year," Isabel said.

"My father wrote to me before he died," I countered.

"If you have some evidence which proves your parentage, I should like very much to see it," Isabel said with a remarkable aplomb which seemed to suggest that she was quite accustomed to dealing with interlopers who appeared on her doorstep bearing letters which they claimed had been sent to them by her dead husband.

I would not be intimidated by her condescending arrogance, no matter how savagely my head throbbed. I said, "I brought my father's letter with me, of course."

Her brows, which were dark and heavy, lifted expectantly above eyes that continued to watch me with that same cool glint of suspicion.

"There was an accident," I continued cautiously. "Somehow, the missive became misplaced in the ensuing scuffle. But I am certain I shall find it soon, in which case I shall certainly present it to you since it proves without a shadow of a doubt that I am Julie McKay, John McKay's legitimate daughter by that first marriage."

"If my husband ever mentioned his child's name to me, I've forgotten it," Isabel said maddeningly. "You must realize how it is for someone in my position, my husband dead, murdered by the very scoundrel who deposited you on my doorstep. No doubt he's there next door this very instant, plotting the next step in his treachery. How am I to know that you aren't involved in some way in his scheme to destroy us?"

"How could I possibly be when it was quite by accident that I met him?" My voice rose in spite of my efforts to control the chagrin to which my stepmother's unyielding attitude had given rise.

There seemed to be no way that I could breach the barriers she had erected against me. Nor was I entirely insensitive to her own dilemma when I recalled how Greg Gallagher had watched me from the bleak shadows beneath the low-hanging gallery as I'd hurried along the crowded street in search of a livery. A wave of dizziness swept over me when I remembered the way his dark eyes had blazed at me, filled with dangerous fires that had sent a sharp surge of alarm racing through my veins. Was Isabel as intimidated by his barely controlled savagery as I had been? Did that explain why she referred to him as a murderer, yet apparently had done nothing to avenge my father's death? The confusion of frightening thoughts danced through my bruised mind, causing the room to spin wildly around me, and I swayed groggily, reaching to grasp the bed's heavily carved footboard in an effort to steady myself.

"But, my dear Julie, you've gone as white as a sheet," Isabel said, moving with a surprising alacrity to assist me as I stumbled to the side of the bed, sinking back gratefully into the thick, feather comforter that folded around me like a smothering, gray cloud.

Chapter SIX

"What is it, Mother?" a woman's voice asked breathlessly. "Who is this person? What's she doing here in our house?"

Our house. I tried to collect my spinning thoughts. But to no avail. It seemed best, then, to yield to the fainting spell, at least for the moment, and I stayed where I was, the woman's frightened voice, followed by Isabel's calmer tones, coming to me from far away, as if they were muffled by the thick layer of down that cradled me.

"I do believe she has succumbed completely," Isabel said. "Go fetch Gertie up from the kitchen, Emma. She'll know what to do."

"Why, it's the same girl I saw riding beside Greg Gallagher in his phaeton," the second voice, which would have been remarkably like Isabel's had it not been for a whining undercurrent of self-pity, said. "I thought to myself at the time that the two of them were up to no good."

"Go, Emma," Isabel ordered impatiently. "It should never do for us to have another death to deal with so soon."

Another death . . . The voices had taken on a nightmarish quality, the second woman saying complainingly, "All right, Mother, if you insist. But I do believe the creature is feigning."

There was a soft, rustling movement and something small and cool touched the tip of my nose, emitting an astringent aroma that seared my throat as I breathed deeply of the aromatic mixture in the smelling bottle that Isabel had thrust beneath my nostrils. I sat up slowly, in time to see a tall, blond man come to a startled halt in the hallway beyond the room's open door. He peered curiously at me, past the ornately carved doorframe, his pale hair disheveled above startled blue eyes whose color was enhanced by an elegant velvet dressing gown that resembled a pelisse, with its fur-trimmed neck and cuffs. Although I was almost totally inexperienced in judging such matters, I could not help noticing that there was a jaded look about his features, which were slightly swollen, as if he had only just recently returned from a prolonged debauch. He was unusually handsome, in spite of his satiated appearance, although I detected a certain weakness about his mouth and chin, which were almost feminine in their delicacy.

"And who might this comely young lady be?" he asked gallantly, squinting a little as he brought his gaze into focus on my face. I guessed that the light spilling in through the tall, narrow windows behind me was painful to his eyes, which looked slightly bleary, bearing out my first impression of him as a man who was overly fond of his nighttime pleasures.

"Greg Gallagher has brought us a visitor," Isabel said.

"Greg?" He gave Isabel a disbelieving stare.

"The man has gall, I must say," Isabel remarked.

"So that's what all of the commotion was about," the blond man said in an abstruse voice. "I heard Emma go rollicking past my door earlier, in a most unladylike fashion, I might add. She'd been up to the tower for some ungodly reason, although she knows how I hate to have my rest disturbed by her bony squeaks and rattlings."

I thought of the sensation I'd had of someone watching from behind the darkly glittering panes of the mansion's cupola when the stagecoach had rattled into town. Had it been Emma I had glimpsed, peering out from behind those regally arched windows?

"She imagined she heard the fire whistles," Isabel said. "She had gone up to the tower room to see if there was smoke rising. If you saw fit to keep respectable hours, you wouldn't be disturbed by the normal activities that are carried out beneath this roof."

"Normal?" The blond man gave a low, scoffing laugh. "It's far more likely that my suspicious-minded sister had gone up there to spy on her highfalutin husband."

"You've no business enticing Renny to join you in your libertine adventures," Isabel retorted.

"It's up to Emma to keep her precious husband at home." The blond man gave a languid shrug of his thin shoulders. I glimpsed decadence plainly written in his face as he continued to watch me in that same brightly feverish way. Yet, oddly enough, I felt strangely intrigued by him.

"A gentleman would not continue to stand there peering into a lady's chamber in such a gawkish manner," Isabel scolded, seemingly reluctant to introduce the two of us.

"The last I recollect, this room was unoccupied," he said lazily, all too apparently taking a certain delight in his own roguishness. "Surely I didn't bring a guest home with me when I returned this morning, a bit the worse for wear, I must admit."

"That will do, Royce," Isabel snapped at him. "This is Julie. She claims to be your stepsister, come all this way from Savannah."

"Julie McKay," I said. "I expected to find my father alive and well or I should never have found the courage to come all this way to Virginia City."

"But you were notified of his death at the time," Royce said. "Mother sent you word of the tragedy. I recall seeing her message myself."

I did not miss the sharp look Isabel shot at him. I guessed then that it had been her intention to trap me in some clever way by suggesting that I was not my father's daughter and thus forcing me to prove myself by presenting her with the evidence she apparently sought. Except that there had been no message from Isabel. Not any that I had seen, and I could not help wondering if Melissa had sought a second hiding place, apart from the jewelry casket where she had hidden my father's letter, in her efforts to keep news of my father from me. But why? Why should my cousin have wanted to keep me in ignorance of the tragedy?

"I received no message," I said in a small, dull voice.

"Do you see now why I must doubt you?" Isabel said. "Why all of us here must maintain a certain reservation toward you? Until you can supply us with some tangible proof of who you are, we can't very well accept you as a member of this family. Your arrival here, in Greg Gallagher's company, has harmed your cause, regardless of what your intentions toward us may eventually prove to be."

"The chances of my having received a message sent all the way from Virginia City are precarious, at best," I said uncertainly.

"That is beside the point now, since it appears that you are here," Royce said. "I propose that, for the time being, at least, you make yourself comfortable. Isabel is noted for her gracious hospitality. You won't find it lacking. It would never do for us to cast you out, thus putting you at the mercy of men like Greg Gallagher. I hasten to assure you that any girl who finds herself abandoned in this town, alone and without suitable accommodation, is almost certain to find herself in a compromising position."

I felt my cheeks flame. "And I assure you, Mr. Ritchie, that I have no intention of imposing myself on your hospitality, if it happens that I am not welcome here in my father's house," I said spiritedly, determined to ignore the pain that thundered behind my temples on that dizzying surge of blood to my face. "I can attend to my own needs in a suitable fashion, if need be."

But inside, my heart was quavering. Where would I go? What would I do if Isabel and the Steps took it upon themselves to decide that I was an impostor, with some wild scheme of her own, whom they could not bring themselves to trust? What would become of me if I failed to locate my father's letter or some other proof that would convince them that I was, indeed, my father's daughter?

It was with a wild surge of relief that I heard Isabel say, "Nonsense. I have never yet begrudged the hospitality of this house to anyone who presents a refined appearance. I can see readily enough that you're a young woman of some breeding. I suppose it's entirely possible that you might yet prove to be John's daughter. Although, as I mentioned to you earlier, that is a fact that remains to be proved."

A thin, pale woman whom I guessed to be several years older than myself brushed past Royce, her drab features plainly agitated. "Gertie seems to have disappeared," she said, coming to an abrupt halt when she saw me seated on the edge of the high, soft bed. "So you've recovered from your little swoon, after all," she remarked coldly.

"My daughter, the Countess Emma Ritchie Caroni," Isabel announced, her chin lifting haughtily. "This is Julie McKay. At least that is who she pretends to be," she added pointedly.

Emma, whose plain face lacked any single distinguishing quality to give it character, hesitated, as if she were not quite certain how to react to my unexpected presence. And I found myself equally at a loss, impressed, in spite of my determination to assume my rightful identity in my father's house, by my stepsister's regal-sounding title.

Rising uncertainly, I executed a shaky curtsy.

Indecision was plainly imprinted on Emma's angular features in that moment when I lifted my head to look squarely at her. Suddenly, her face seemed vaguely familiar and I found myself thinking that it was a face I had seen numerous times before, along the streets of Savannah or at social functions held in the big houses along the river that were a part of my childhood memories. Not like the pert features of the flamboyant, fox-faced girl on the stage, or even my own countenance, which had a full, wide mouth and a nose that turned up slightly at its tip, set beneath eyes that were their own unique shade of green. Like my cousin Melissa, the Countess Emma Ritchie Caroni was decidedly plain.

Now, as I became increasingly conscious of Royce's libertine stare, I caught myself questioning the desirability of good looks in a place like Virginia City, which swarmed with unattached males whose way of life had enhanced their natural aggressiveness and sense of competition in a manner that quite frankly dismayed me. I had been exposed before to men who viewed pretty women as prizes. But none, so far, had watched me quite so passionately as Greg Gallagher had done, nor had I encountered any who were as boldly flirtatious as Royce appeared to be. Or was he bent on teasing me, as he had teased Isabel with his shameless suggestion that he might very well have been accompanied by a vivacious companion upon his return from his late revels? His implication had been unmistakable and wickedly intriguing. Which was precisely as he had intended it to be, I thought when he flashed me a sly little smile that seemed to imply some mutual understanding.

I glanced quickly at Emma, who was saying to me in a querulous voice, "You have some identification, of course."

"It was my intention to present you with a letter from my father upon my arrival here," I said.

"Was?" A flicker of doubt flashed behind Emma's pale eyes.

"It seems there has been an accident," Isabel told her.

"A team bolted," I said. "Greg Gallagher's team, as a matter of fact, which explains why he felt obligated to drive me up here. I was struck down in the street, which accounts for my disheveled appearance. My reticule flew from my hand and it was only later, after Dr. Quinn had examined me to make certain nothing was broken, that I managed to recover it. Apparently the letter I spoke of was lost in the melee and it didn't occur to me to search for it in the street when I left Dr. Quinn's office. I had received a rather stiff blow that left my senses reeling. But I feel quite recovered now and perhaps, under the circumstances, it might be wise for me to do that now. I had tucked what money I had left into the envelope." My voice trailed off uncertainly.

"What you suggest is out of the question," Isabel said. "In the event that you are John's daughter, we can't have you pawing around in the dust and horse dung like riffraff, not to mention those chattering little Chinamen who scrabble after the chunks of ore that fall off of the wagons. If the letter and your money are there, someone will find them and return them to you. Whatever else the men in this town may be, they're basically honest."

"That is, unless the miner who happens to recover your little hoard finds himself desperately in need of a new grubstake," Royce contributed in his lazy way, showing no inclination to return to his bed. "In which case his basic honesty may manifest itself six months or a year from now, if he's lucky enough to strike it rich. You may end up a millionairess yet, little stepsister, since any man who struck it rich on your money would feel compelled to cut you in for a share of his claim."

"I suppose that's your real reason for coming here, isn't it?" Emma asked accusingly. "To attempt to claim a share of the proceeds from the sale of the mine, on the pretense of having been related to John McKay. Just because Royce likes to tease is no reason for you to assume that we're willing to accept you."

"I came here to see my father," I said.

"A daring undertaking for a young girl alone," Isabel commented. "I take it that you are now without funds."

I nodded. "But not without means altogether," I said quickly, my chin lifting. "I'm an experienced accountant. I'm certain I can find a reliable position in one of the mine offices, should it come to that."

"But that would be unthinkable," Emma gasped, giving me an appalled stare. "Common! We can't have you making yourself common, if you're to remain here with us." She jerked her gaze away from me, her pale eyes beseeching Isabel. "Mother, imagine what Renaldo would say, were we to allow anyone even remotely associated with the family to become a tradesman, least of all someone who claims she's Father's own blood relation! It makes no real difference whether she is Julie McKay or not, if you insist on taking her in."

"Your precious Renny has had his own dealings with the tradespeople," Royce remarked in his mischievous way. "I doubt that he'd be all that horrified, although he might very well pretend that his royal sensitivities had been insulted."

"Just because you choose to dally away your time on sporting row with the likes of that trashy Julia Bulette is no reason to suspect that Renaldo shares your low tastes," Emma said coldly. But I could not help noticing that her plain features had become oddly distorted by an underlying savagery.

"Do you think that I don't know why you climb up to the tower room so often? And at the oddest hours," Royce added suggestively. "It makes a most convenient watchtower, doesn't it, Emma, darling, where you can go to spy on Renaldo without his guessing what you're up to. If Renny were the pure-hearted gallant you make him out to be, there would be no need for you to go creaking off up there to look for him, would there? Perhaps, then, I could get the rest I deserve."

Emma's face had reddened, and her eyes, which were the color of ladyfinger grapes, threatened to burst from her head. "Why must you taunt me in this wretched manner, Royce?" she demanded in a voice that had grown thin with self-pity. "Why must you debase Renaldo by speaking of him in such a reprehensible manner? If I climb up to the tower room, it's for the same reason you yourself choose to go up there. There can be no harm in that, can there?"

"I've asked all four of you to discontinue your visits to the tower room," Isabel said. "I find your reasons for going up there extremely inelegant. I won't have the members of this household indulging their bad taste."

I sensed that whatever strange mission drew the four Steps to the odd little cupola perched on top of the mansion, Isabel preferred not to discuss it in my presence, beyond her veiled reference to "bad taste," with the result that I found myself growing more curious than I might ordinarily have been about the family my father had adopted as his own when he'd married Isabel.

"Whatever your own reasons for climbing to the top of this melancholy pile of timbers and stone, you surely don't imagine that Renny's nocturnal meanderings are entirely innocent, do you, Emma, darling?" Royce persisted, in spite of the warning look Isabel turned on him.

"Renaldo seldom leaves the house at all," Emma shot back at him, suddenly turning pale.

I glimpsed fear in her eyes, above lips that had suddenly

begun to quiver. Spinning away from Royce's taunting smile, she darted into the shadows, and an instant later I heard a door close with a loud slam in a distant part of the house.

"You should go to her and apologize for your rude behavior," Isabel said to Royce, who seemed oddly detached, almost oblivious to Emma's distress, as if he had had no part in it.

I thought how bored they all must be as a result of the tremendous wealth that had given them a false sense of superiority, so that they felt compelled to hold themselves aloof from the trials and tribulations that beset ordinary people. Had my father been possessed by that same callously vulgar sense of sovereignty after he had made his big strike and achieved the wealth and prestige that had enabled him to erect a mansion equal in size and grandeur to New York's finest houses? Had he taken offense at some chance remark Greg Gallagher had made and called the man out, as I had seen dandies do back home in Savannah? Was that the real reason he had been "murdered," as Isabel seemed almost to delight in putting it? As if she held some personal grudge against Greg and was determined, because of it, to cast aspersions on his character, I could not help thinking. "They sold out to me after the vein went dry," Greg had said to me. What had he meant to imply?

My head started to swim again.

"I'll leave you alone now to rest," Isabel said kindly. "It's plain to see you've been mishandled."

"It was an accident," I murmured feebly, aware, even as I spoke, that it was myself I hoped to convince.

"I, for one, sincerely doubt that," Isabel stated bluntly.

I stared up numbly into her plump face, which was not without its own softening qualities, for all of the granite determination that glittered behind her dark eyes.

"Why do you say that?" I heard myself asking.

"Greg is the best driver on the lode, everyone in town knows that," she said in that same artless way. "Those handsome bays of his would stand up on their hind hooves and dance for him, if he gave them the word."

"What are you trying to tell me?" I whispered dizzily,

visualizing all too clearly that lean, dark form unfurling his whip with deadly precision and a horse's gleaming rump marred by a crusted streak of dried blood.

"That Greg Gallagher is wholly unpredictable and not a man to be trifled with," Isabel said.

"How did my father die?" I asked numbly.

"My husband met his death at the mine," Isabel said with a strange stoicism. "A piece of drill steel was dropped on him while he was lowering himself in the cage. It pierced the top of his skull, pinning him to the plank floor. Tim was there when they brought him out."

"Tim?" I echoed in a horrified whisper.

"My son. You'll meet him later. Perhaps Marcus will be here, as well. I have three sons and one daughter," Isabel added succinctly.

I was only vaguely aware of her disentangling implication, my thoughts arrested by her horrifying description of my father's death.

"He had gone to the mine alone?" I heard myself asking in a faint voice.

"He went there frequently. His habits were well known. He was never a man to relegate his responsibilities as owner of the mine to underlings."

I glanced at the mansion next door, looking at it through the fine filaments of the expensive curtains that served to soften the evil glare of its darkly shuttered windows.

"I can't imagine why anyone would have wanted to harm my father," I said. "He was never the kind of man to inspire treachery in others."

"You are being presumptuous," Isabel said flatly. "Those of us here were well aware that Greg had been trying to talk John into selling out to him for some time. When he refused, Greg found his own means to acquire the property he coveted and which, by no small coincidence, happens to border his own claim." My stepmother's voice had turned decidedly bitter and there were acid lines etched at the corners of her small mouth.

"But you didn't have to sell out to him," I said. "No one could have forced you to do that."

"It seemed the opportune thing to do at the time," Isabel said.

Chapter SEVEN

I settled insecurely into the uncertain routine of my father's house. I had broken my ties with Uncle Grant and Aunt Hillary when I embarked on the long journey that had brought me eventually to the lively mining metropolis located high in the Washoe Mountains and, as tentative as my relationship with them had so far proved itself to be, Isabel and the Steps were all I had.

My unfortunate encounter with Greg Gallagher, compounded by the shattering news of my father's tragic death, had left me shaken and I was content to spend the larger share of the next few days in the room Isabel had assigned to me, while I waited as patiently as I could for the debilitating ache in my bruised temples to gradually subside. In spite of her aloofness and her continued determination not to accept me as John McKay's daughter, at least until I had succeeded in producing the proof she required, my stepmother was kind enough, affording me the generous hospitality that she considered to be the just due of any guest beneath her roof.

As for the others, I had not yet made up my mind about them, having sensed an indecisiveness in them all that I was wholly at a loss to explain, beyond the fact that they were apparently waiting to take their cue from Isabel who, I had quickly discovered, reigned over the bustling household like a dowager queen.

The room Isabel had given me was large and comfortable. I found it a pleasant enough place to while away the tedious hours as I waited for the fits of dizziness—the aftermath of the blow I'd received from Greg's prancing horses—to pass. A bath, far grander than anything I had ever seen, with its imported bronze fixtures, was located only a short distance down the hall, and although water was a scarcity in the mining town, I was afforded the luxury of a pleasant soak my first night at the mansion, submerged beneath fragrantly scented billows of Gertie's hard-milled, honey-and-cornmeal soap.

An upholstered setee, its mahogany frame tortured into the latest curlicues and scrolls, stood before the bay window, and I found it convenient to recline against the thick velvet bolsters that padded the seat's carved arms when I was seized by one of my attacks. Staring out into the gently waving branches of the poplar and locust trees, I told myself that it was the small, bright-yellow and black birds that had built a swinging nest on one of the branches that held my attention. But in fact it was Greg Gallagher's mansion, with its secretively guarded windows, that interested me most. I had come, during those quiet hours of watching, to believe that the house situated below my father's mansion held the proof I needed to establish myself as a deserving member of Isabel's household, for I could not forget that it had been Greg Gallagher who had found my reticule, following the incident that had very nearly cost me my life. Although several days had passed, no one had appeared at the mansion with the missing letter from my father and the last of my meager funds. Under the circumstances, it did not seem unreasonable to assume that Greg had confiscated the letter for his own dire reasons, just as I had first suspected.

Once or twice I had caught a glimpse of his lean form disappearing into the tightly shuttered house next door, and on several occasions I had seen a spare, middle-aged woman, whom I assumed to be the housekeeper he'd told me about, scurrying between the house and the laundry shed that stood at the rear of the shallow lot, near the carriage house and stable. A small Chinese man, dismayingly similar to Isabel's Sam, inhabited the low-roofed shed that was plainly visible through the thin branches of the trees and from which thick billows of steam erupted from time to time, attesting to the sudsy labors of the wiry little Chinese man.

I could not dismiss from my mind those times when, upon hearing a horse approaching Greg's house late at night, I had risen quickly from my bed to peer out into the darkness, in time to see Dr. Quinn dismount in the street below and make his way unsteadily up the stone steps that were guarded on either side by the same spear-headed spikes that enclosed the small, front garden. Watching him disappear, on those occasions, into the black shadows at the front of the Gallagher mansion, I was aware of something stealthy in his demeanor, as if it were his intention to go undetected into that secretively shuttered house that intrigued me more than I would have wished it to because of Greg's presence there.

"Greg Gallagher and Thomas Quinn have a great deal in common," Isabel told me when I remarked to her one morning on Dr. Quinn's frequent visits to the house next door.

"Are you referring to Dr. Quinn's fondness for spirits?" I asked, recalling the betraying aroma that had clung to his person the day he had attended to my bruises.

"Among other things," Isabel said obscurely. "Not that their indulgences are to be held against them. My husband enjoyed his evening out at one of the more refined establishments for gentlemen as much as the next man. That was to be expected. And it wasn't the same as if he had patronized the one-bitters that cater to the teamsters and muckers and drifters. The more elegant establishments have their carved rosewood and mahogany, with fine crystal and plate-glass mirrors. I fault no man for taking advantage of what few small pleasures are available in a place like this. Not even Greg Gallagher."

For a moment or two Isabel sounded almost nostalgic; there was a certain commonness lurking beneath her sophisticated gloss that surprised me. I had the peculiar impression that the refinement she went to such pains to display, in both her dress and her manner, was merely a thin veneer that had threatened, if only briefly, to crack and expose a solidly earthy being hiding inside the drab, black widow's weeds that she continued to wear even though my father had been dead for more than a year.

I dressed carefully for my first appearance at dinner with the family, slipping on one of Melissa's more elegant castoffs, a town gown of levantine folice' in raisin d'Espagne, a color that had been the vogue since the late fifties, over my plain linen shift and pantaloons. Pulling and puffing my auburn tresses into an artful arrangement that satisfactorily concealed the purple bruises at my temples, I ventured forth, intent on making an impression befitting the station I was determined to assume as a daughter of the house.

As I made my way carefully down the broadly sweeping staircase, I deliberately refrained from dwelling on the possibility that there was a hidden legacy that belonged to me. While I rested in my room, recuperating from the bumps and bruises I had suffered in my encounter with Greg Gallagher's spirited team of bays, I had tried more than once to imagine what could possibly have happened to the signed document my father had mentioned in his letter. Why had I not been notified by his attorneys that he had seen fit to bequeath me some small share of his fortune? Had Isabel mentioned the legacy he had wanted me to have in the message she claimed she had sent to me upon his death? Had my father given the document to her for safekeeping until such time as I might come to claim it for myself? In which case, would she see fit to produce it when she became convinced that I was indeed John McKay's rightful daughter, as she must surely do when I had succeeded in providing the proof she required to establish my identity?

Gathering the voluminous skirts of Melissa's gown around limbs that had suddenly turned to water, I could not help wondering how I was going to succeed in proving myself to Isabel and the Steps. Nor could I refrain from considering the possible consequences if such proof failed to be forthcoming. Where would I go? What would I do? In spite of the courageous boasts I had made about being equipped to look after myself, I found that I was frightened. In the face of those chilling doubts there seemed to be only one thing for me to do: I would seek out Greg Gallagher and openly confront him. If he proved unwilling to reveal to me the truth about my father's missing letter and the few dollars it had contained, there was always the slight possibility that he might give himself away. If he did, I decided on reckless impulse, I would search out the letter for myself. It would be a comparatively simple matter to slip down the slope of the garden to the house next door in the dead of night, although I did not doubt for an instant that such an undertaking would prove to be highly dangerous.

Yet, in my desperation to convince Isabel and the Steps, whose guarded reticence troubled me more than I cared to admit, the half-formulated plan provided me with a pin-point glimmer of hope so that as I entered the huge dining room I was able to smile tentatively at the group assembled around the mammoth table that, like the mansion, was dominated by Isabel.

Emma's husband, Count Renaldo Caroni, whom the others referred to familiarly as "Renny," was the first to rise from one of the thronelike chairs when I stepped between thick, sliding doors that, like the rest of the house, attested to Isabel's wildly lavish spending sprees at a time when the river of rich ore spilling out of the McKay-Ritchie Mine had held a false promise of perpetual wealth.

"Ah, it's the lovely, titian-haired Julie, consenting to join us at last at the family board," Renny said in his highly affected English, bowing from the waist and coming forward to touch the tips of my fingers to his thin, dry lips. "*Buona sera*, Julie. I am reminded suddenly of Giorgione. You are familiar with his works, surely. I find that you bear a rather shocking resemblance to his Venus reclining in a landscape. Incidentally, the *Sleeping Venus* was the first painting executed by one of my fellow countrymen to find its way into the Dresden Gallery."

"I'm afraid I have never had an opportunity to visit Europe," I said.

"A pity," Renny murmured, his fingers lingering cloyingly on my arm as he guided me to my chair.

Beyond his elegantly clad presence, I saw Emma watching me, her pale eyes gleaming like glass marbles in the midst of her pasty features, and I could not help thinking that the match was an incongruous one, to say the least.

I had met the others, who were present only briefly when they had paused at the door to my room, in Isabel's company, on the presumption of being introduced to their current houseguest. But I had not missed the curiosity that had seethed behind the studiously sophisticated looks both Tim and Marcus Ritchie had turned on me when Isabel told them who I was, nor did I believe for a moment that they were as uninterested in my reasons for being there as they had tried to pretend.

Marcus, my stepbrother, said, half-rising from his place at the head of the long table, "It's gratifying to see you are finally up to joining us, Julie. I've reserved a place for you here next to me, in anticipation of this momentous event."

Julie. Not Miss McKay. Just Julie. On Renny's sharply angled elbow, I gravitated toward the place Marcus indicated, a queasy sensation sweeping over me as a tiny jab of pain darted through my temples. What was in their minds? Why were they so determined to make me feel unwanted in my father's house? What had they to gain by denying me my rightful place among them?

Chapter EIGHT

I said, "I've often wondered what it would be like to assume my rightful place at my father's table. This is a moment I've often dreamed of."

A chilling silence enveloped the room, freezing Isabel's small smile into place, turning Tim's frankly curious stare to stone. While Royce's open appraisal of me became mischievously leering, his brows quirked wickedly above his slightly glazed eyes, as if, in spite of the early hour, he had imbibed too freely of the amber spirits that twinkled in the crystal goblet beside his plate.

Renny's richly accented voice invaded the cold silence, its soft tones falling warmly around me. "We are, as they say here, birds of a feather," he commented. "That is to say, we are both johnny-come-latelys to this godforsaken place with all of its *esagerato* opulence."

Esagerato. It was not difficult for me to derive the meaning of the unfamiliar term when I had been seated next to Marcus and could take time to look around me while we waited for Gertie to appear in response to Isabel's impatient tap on the small, silver bell that matched the gleaming, monogrammed table service.

A French clock decorated with bronze figures stood between exquisite Holland vases on the marble mantel that dominated one wall of the large room, while overhead, a Czechoslovakian rock-crystal chandelier had been lighted, its glittering drops shooting bright shards of light down on our heads.

The room's furnishings were of mellowed walnut, the burled wood glistening beneath layers of scented beeswax that enhanced its rich patina so that the shimmer of Viennese crystal was clearly caught in the polished surface of the huge sideboard whose back pediment and doors were handcarved in a bold pheasant pattern.

I saw at a glance that Isabel had spared no expense in her efforts to enhance the spacious rooms of the big house my father had built for her with the mine's earnings.

"Does it meet with your approval, Julie dear?" Royce's slightly blurred voice cut short my speculations concerning the probable cost of the room's furnishings.

"I'd seen descriptions of the house in the Eastern press," I remarked, aware even as I spoke that I had succeeded once again in saying the wrong thing.

It was Emma who gave voice to the seething doubts that were plainly written on all of their faces, with the exceptions of Royce and Renny, both of whom regarded me with a tolerant amusement that I knew, for all of my limited experience, could quickly burgeon into a daring flirtatiousness were I to give either of them the least encouragement.

"The press gave away a good many pertinent details describing our personal lives," Emma was saying. "I don't doubt for a minute that you arrived here well informed."

"Not as well informed as I would like to be, seeing that I am a part of this family," I retorted, a sudden agitation edging my voice so that it rose an octave above its normal pitch, making me sound decidedly shrewish. "Please forgive me," I went on quickly, in a belated effort to retrieve myself. "I'm not as fully recovered from the accident as I had hoped."

"You still persist in your efforts to convince us that you are John's daughter," Isabel commented.

"There is no effort involved, since that is, in fact, who I happen to be," I stated, relieved to see Gertie approaching through the swinging door that led to the kitchen wing, bearing a steaming Meissen tureen in her work-stained hands.

I had already learned that Isabel frowned on what she referred to as "idle gossip" among the servants and, as a consequence, family conversations invariably ceased whenever the plumply rosy Irish-born housekeeper put in an appearance.

Nevertheless, I could not help thinking, as I watched her move silently to serve us, that Gertie was as wholly aware of all that transpired within those four walls as anyone present, with the exception of me. Although her smooth features wore a dull, indifferent expression, her eyes were witty, glowing between their crinkled lids with an avaricious curiosity. Given ample opportunity, I suspected that Gertie would talk a streak; envisioned her participation in private, backfence conclaves with Greg Gallagher's housekeeper, whose name, I had learned since coming to the mansion, was Bertha Foster.

Little by little, I was gleaning bits and pieces of information about the two houses that stood side by side on the steep slopes of Sun Mountain, my father's mansion taking precedence over the mansion that stood slightly below it on the sharply terraced street.

"You are from the South, then," Marcus remarked when Gertie had gone.

"Surely Father told you he was from Savannah," I said.

Marcus flashed me a gallant smile, his blondly slender good looks reminding me of the blades who had come to call on Cousin Melissa out of some deeply imbred sense of duty. For the most part, I had found their gentle flattery dull and unexciting. Even before I had uncovered the letter from my father, I had wanted far more from life than was available to me as Uncle Grant's ward.

Now, as Marcus continued to regard me in that same chivalrous way, as if I were not his stepsister at all, but yet another empty-headed female who succumbed much too readily to fainting spells and male flattery, it occurred to me for the first time that my position here in my father's house would be no different from what it had been before. If Isabel and her brood accepted me at all, it would be as a poor relation they had begrudgingly taken in, and, unless I could find a way to claim the legacy my father had promised me in the missing letter, I would have no choice but to accept their charity.

"Father never spoke to us of his past life," Emma was saying.

"Surely he made some mention of it in casual conversation," I said.

"Briefly, perhaps," Emma conceded, glancing at Isabel, who said, "His memories of those times were bitter. It seemed that his first wife's sister wanted the child that had been of that marriage, and forbade him to contact her. He seemed content enough to leave it at that. Particularly since he had severed all ties he had with the past to make a new beginning for himself here."

Severed all ties. . . . The words, spoken in Isabel's studiously polite tones, tore at me and I said defensively, "If that had been his true intention, I should never have heard from him again."

Tim, who appeared in some respects to be counterpart to both Royce and Marcus, in spite of his dark coloring and muscular miner's body, looked up sharply from his soup plate. "Father contacted you, then?" His eyes, which were as dark as Greg Gallagher's but lacked the smoldering inner fire that had burned so brightly behind Greg's piercing stare, were frankly doubting.

"I received a letter from him," I said carefully. "Otherwise, I shouldn't be here at all."

"You took your time in coming, I must say," Emma said primly.

"Must we be so gloomy," Renny said. "Julie is here. What else can possibly matter now? The past is gone. *Defunto. Una perdita assoluta!*"

Detecting a note of bitterness in his voice, I said, "Perhaps we all find ourselves in a position, at one time or another in our lives, when we are left with no alternative other than to strike out in a new direction."

"You are not only beautiful, but wise," Renny said, his dark eyes glistening suddenly with moisture. "It is not always an easy thing to do, but when circumstances dictate, one has no choice, does one?" He shrugged, gesturing helplessly with hands that were as frail and white as a woman's. "Mine is a noble heritage. My family was among the *nobiltà* who were put to flight in 1848, during a revolutionary outbreak against the rulers of Parma and Modena. Had it not been for our darling Isabella, I should still be impoverished, through no fault of my own, of course." Raising his glass, which contained a deep, sparkling wine brought by freight wagon from the vineyards north of San Francisco, Renny turned his moist gaze on Isabel. *"Una fortuna inattesa,"* he toasted her. "Had it not been for you and your dear Emma, I should be moldering away in abject poverty in some ill-attended villa."

"What Renny is attempting to tell you, Julie darling, is that he was bought and paid for by McKay-Ritchie money," Royce remarked with a poorly feigned innocence. "I believe the proper term to describe someone like our dear Renaldo is 'gigolo.' Poor Mother. She got more than she bargained for when she propositioned Renny, in Emma's behalf. My esteemed brother-in-law has rather expensive tastes, I fear."

Emma turned a wildly beseeching look on Isabel, her grape-green eyes bulging in watery indignation, while Renny darted a startled look between the three of them, pretending that he had failed to grasp the gist of Royce's shocking revelation.

"I suggest you forgo drinking brandy with your dinner, after this, if you can't control your tongue," Isabel said sharply, turning scornful eyes on Royce. "I won't have Emma or our guest insulted in such a manner."

"It's purely a matter of 'look who's calling the kettle black,' in any case," Marcus said dryly, flashing me a bored little smile. "Both Royce and Renny have expensive tastes, which helps to explain the paucity of service in this household. Mother was forced to let the servants go, with the exception of Gertie and Sam, when the mine failed."

"We make do," Isabel said shortly.

"I understand you've already had the dubious pleasure of meeting our neighbor, Greg Gallagher," Marcus continued. "No doubt he told you that he is the new owner of the McKay-Ritchie. With the exception of Tim's claim,

I might add. Were it not for good old Tim here, we might find ourselves in rather difficult straits, financially speaking. One grows accustomed to having unlimited amounts of money to spend. It's not easy as you might imagine to cope with life's unexpected little exigencies when the well suddenly goes dry."

"But surely Greg Gallagher paid you handsomely for the mine," I said.

"He got it for a steal," Tim said gloomily.

"Not to hear Greg tell it," Marcus said. "He's spread the word all over town that we deliberately tricked him into believing that the main ore body was, as yet, untapped."

"Didn't you?" Royce asked candidly.

"The specimens he found in the mine were genuine enough," Marcus said.

"Except that you had no idea where they came from," Royce said. He turned to me. "It's what is known as salting a mine. Father had left some odd bits and pieces of jewelry-grade ore lying around the assay house. It was easy enough for Marcus and Tim to transport those bins of rich rock into the mine, where they dumped their contents for Greg to find when he inspected the lower levels, prior to buying the controlling interest in the McKay-Ritchie. It was one of the few mines left on the lode where stocks were still selling by the foot. Greg was rabid to grab them all up, after he had tested enough of the ore my brothers dumped there to convince him that the mine was still productive, in spite of rumors that it had started to go dry."

"Where else could the ore have come from, if not the McKay-Ritchie?" Isabel challenged Royce. "The vein is there and it's up to Greg to find it, now that the mine belongs to him."

It was true then. Greg Gallagher was the new owner of the mine, just as he had told me. Furthermore, I had begun to suspect that he had sufficient reason for accusing Isabel and the Steps of misleading him, in the face of what Royce had just revealed.

"Where is the mine located?" I asked almost timidly, confronted by the sudden unsavory prospect that my presence in the house might very well prove to be an intolerable burden now that Isabel no longer owned a share in the mine that had provided my father and his adoptive family with a more than ample livelihood for nearly a decade. Did that perhaps explain, at least in part, why they refused to acknowledge me as my father's daughter? I could not help wondering.

"There are stopes and shafts all over Sun Mountain," Marcus said, gesturing broadly. "The main entrance is a quarter-mile from here, however."

"Is that where it happened?" I heard myself asking in that same small voice, as if by making myself as inconspicuous as possible, I thought reproachfully, I could somehow lessen the threat I was suddenly certain I must pose to a security that was precariously balanced, to say the least, if it were true that Isabel had been forced to let her servants go for a lack of funds to pay their wages.

"Yes, if you're referring to Father's murder," Emma said, her voice turning oddly vicious. "We're well off rid of the mine," she went on in that same strangely vehement way.

"My beautiful wife cannot tolerate dark places," Renny said, his unfortunate choice of words mocking Emma's plainness, whether or not that was what he had intended to do.

"I've seen *her* there," Emma said hoarsely, her pinched features suddenly turning pale.

She looked accusingly at Renny, daring him with that icy stare to deny that what she had said was true.

"Would it shock you too much to learn that Virginia City has a ghost?" Royce said to me. I realized then that I was staring at Emma in frank perplexity.

"I doubt that anything I learn about this place could shock me overly much," I remarked in an effort to disguise my curiosity.

"There has always been a great deal of superstition connected with the mine," Isabel said. "You have to realize that the majority of the men who worked for us came here from abroad. They were illiterate, for the most part, Cornishmen and the Irish who have their tommy knockers and other spooks they claimed haunted the tunnels."

"Isabel has always resented the fact that John would

not allow her to enter the McKay-Ritchie tunnels," Renny said.

"The men would have walked out on us if she'd tried to go beyond the base of the main shaft," Marcus said. "As it was, she had to content herself with riding up and down in the cage, which was a risk in itself, to hear some of them tell it. I suppose it's only natural for men who place their lives in jeopardy to seek a scapegoat whenever one of them dies due to his own carelessness."

"It doesn't always happen that way," Tim objected. "Mining is a hazardous occupation, at best, particularly in these cruel hills."

"Hazardous or not, some of them claimed it was Isabel who brought them bad luck," Royce said. He turned his attention toward his mother. "Do you suppose it's actually possible that those little visits of yours caused the vein to play out?"

"If anyone brought bad luck to the McKay-Ritchie, it was Loryea Labree," Emma said, her pale stare switching away from Renny's dapper countenance to focus unyieldingly on Marcus. "I suspect that Marcus may have taken her there without any of us knowing it," she went on in that same, unforgiving voice. "Maybe he saw it as a way to impress Loryea when it became apparent to him that Greg had begun to take an interest in her."

In the next moment, Gertie reappeared to place a platter on which a cold duck reposed, quivering inside a clear, gelatinous mass, before Marcus, who whetted the shimmering blade of the long, silver carving knife that lay beside his plate and began to carve, seemingly indifferent to Emma's chilling accusation.

"You know as well as I do that Loryea was attracted to a great many men," Marcus said when Gertie had gathered up our soup plates and was gone.

"Tom Quinn certainly made no secret of his infatuation with her," Isabel said to Emma. "It's unfair of you to try to link Marcus' name to that particular tragedy. After all, he is your brother."

"I was only trying to determine why our good fortune fell through the way it did," Emma said lamely.

"Not very realistically, I'm afraid," Isabel stated.

"You can't deny that she's been seen since the . . .

accident," Emma persisted, the slight hesitation in her voice instantly alerting me.

"Must we go into the details of Loryea's death over supper," Royce protested. "Hers was a particularly heinous murder, to say the least."

"No one mentioned murder," Emma hissed.

"Nevertheless, all of us here are aware that that is what it amounted to, with the exception of Julie, perhaps."

Murder. First my father. And now the woman named Loryea Labree. Was it something more than a coincidence that she too had known Greg Gallagher? More shattering still, was the attempt that had been made on my own life yet another deliberately planned sequence in that chilling chain of events, because I happened to be John McKay's daughter?

Or was I leaping to conclusions? Emma had referred to Loryea Labree's death in that strangely hesitant way as an "accident," just as my father's death could also be termed accidental. There was, as yet, no real proof that it had been otherwise. It was Isabel and the Steps who insisted that it had been murder, because of their own unsatisfactory dealings with Greg Gallagher.

I said, "People seem to have a habit of dying unexpectedly in this place."

"In Loryea's case, I suspect she brought it on herself," Royce said. "There had been rumors floating around town for some time that she had taken a secret lover, a man of some consequence, whom she was meeting clandestinely. It was hinted, following her bizarre death, that he had destroyed her in an effort to protect himself from scandal."

He did not have to mention names for me to guess that he was referring to Greg Gallagher. I shivered, remembering how Greg's dark gaze had burned into me from beneath the balustraded gallery that overhung the town's narrow street, never wavering from my face, as if he were determined to draw me against my will into his own mysterious intrigues.

Suddenly, there was not the least doubt in my mind that he had known, in some mysterious way, that I would be on the afternoon stage that day and had deliberately stationed himself there to watch for me.

Chapter NINE

Back in my room, I fell into a deep depression. Blaming my malaise on the laudanum Dr. Quinn had given me, and which I had dutifully taken to alleviate the pain in my temple, I decided that what I needed to clear my head and restore my appetite, which had not done justice to the thick, glossy slices of galantine that, I had gathered from Isabel's comments at dinner, Gertie had taken it upon herself to concoct, using a canvasback duck in lieu of tender-breasted capon, was a brisk walk in the clear, mountain air. Although it had already grown quite late, I knew that there would be a moon later to light my way along the pale tracks that passed by the mansion and wound through the cemetery. Several times during the past few days I had ventured from my room late at night to stand before the tall windows at the end of the second-floor hallway, staring out into the fitful moonlight at the ornate tomb that, according to Isabel, my father had built into the mountain some years earlier when the only child she had been able to give him had been born dead. The tomb presented a substantial testimony to the permanence of his life in the isolated mining town where death was accepted with a resolute stoicism and that had a half-dozen cemeteries scattered above it across the somber slopes of the mountain.

Venturing down to Gertie's darkened kitchen, I found a lantern standing in readiness on a high shelf in the adjoining pantry, its glass globe gleaming above a wick that had been freshly trimmed. Tucking a plentiful supply of matches into the pocket of my gown, I slipped quietly out through the back door into the garden.

The mansion loomed darkly above me, save for a feeble flickering of light that seeped between the heavily scalloped side curtains of one of the second-floor rooms. Darting past one of the thick chains that tied the big house to the steep slopes of the mountain, I glanced upward at the tower room, wondering if Emma or one of the others was there, shrouded in darkness, carrying out some forbidden ritual which taxed my imagination.

That other house, situated directly below my father's on its own stony outcropping, was sheathed in darkness. Beyond it, the town itself presented an exciting panorama of flickering candles and gas lamps. Tantalizing strains of tinny music rose faintly from the darkly clustered buildings tucked into the midst of the palely looming tailing piles, carried upward on the unmistakable sounds of masculine revelry.

Picking my way carefully past the pungent patches of sage and rioting sprigs of rabbit brush that threatened to encroach on Isabel's zealously tended garden, I set off along an overgrown wagon track that was still faintly visible in the deepening dusk, heading toward the marble colonnade that supported the balustraded cornice my father had used to decorate the impressive tomb. The opening beneath the monument, which had been patterned after a Grecian temple, yawned like an open mouth against the pale face of the mountain, above rows of marching headstones that were ranked below it like a vigilantly watchful vanguard.

A short while later I stepped bravely into the deep shadows beneath the cornice, fumbling in my pocket for one of the matches and touching it with nervous fingers to the lantern's oil-soaked wick. The orange flame leaped up, streaking the chimney with smoke. Turning it down to a steady tongue of fire, I clamped the glass globe firmly into place and, holding the lantern high, pried loose the bar that secured the ornate, iron doors.

Bracing the doors wide with heavy chunks of loose rock that I found lying nearby, I stepped gingerly into the vault that had been hollowed into the mountainside, its interior walled with smoothly dressed blocks of granite that glittered with fool's gold in the pale glow from my lantern.

Almost as if guided by some unseen power, I found myself gravitating unerringly toward my father's casket, which had been placed inside a rectangular opening between the thick stones, its scrolled silver handle visible behind a thick, beveled-glass window. A small brass plaque bolted to the glass gave my father's name and the dates of his birth and death.

A second casket, much smaller than the first, occupied a nearby space, the plaque attached to its glass window bearing the name, Martin John McKay, above an inscription that identified the miniature remains as those of Isabel's stillborn son. I took a melancholy satisfaction in knowing that, although the child who would have been my half-brother had not lived, he had been named for my father. What had my father's feelings been when he had learned that his infant son would never know life? Had some part of him died, as well? Had he planned for the child who would one day have been his heir, if he had lived? Had the death of that child prompted him, in the end, to pen the letter that Melissa had hidden from me in her jewelry casket and that now appeared to be lost to me forever, unless I could find a way to retrieve it?

Going to stand once more before my father's casket, behind its thick window of glass, I beseeched him to speak to me; to direct me to the legacy that he had wanted me to have. I had had enough of being the poor relation. Surely the legacy would be large enough to enable me to pay my own way. It came to me with a sudden certainty, as I stood before the gleaming, silver casket sealed behind the leaded panel of glass, that that was what my father had intended. He had surely guessed, when he read Aunt Hillary's letter commanding him never to try to contact me again following his marriage to Isabel, that my life as a member of Uncle Grant's war-impoverished household was far from happy. Not that I had been ungrateful to Uncle Grant and Aunt Hillary for all they had done for me and my ailing mother while she lived. But they had afforded us their charity grudgingly, an attitude that must surely have made itself known through Aunt Hillary's tersely penned reprimands, if, as I had done when his own letter came belatedly into my hands, my father had taken time to read between the lines.

"Father?" The softly imploring sound of my voice was quickly swallowed up by the dim reaches of the huge tomb. "Father, please help me. I've missed you so these many long years. I need you. Father?"

The terrible, unanswering silence of the cavernous vault closed around me and I turned away despairingly.

The answer to my softly spoken plea, when it finally came, manifested itself in the midst of my own troubled thoughts. I had started back toward the vault's iron doors when suddenly it occurred to me, as if in answer to my softly spoken implorations, that I must call on my father's attorneys at the first available opportunity, and I was certain then that my father had heard me in my abject desperation and had made his reply known to me.

Immediately my spirits lifted and I hurried on light feet toward the vault's entrance, wondering why I had not thought sooner of going to his attorneys, aware even as the question crossed my mind that it had been because I'd been too grievously distracted by news of my father's death, following as it had in the wake of the accident, to think clearly. At the thought of those swiftly plunging horses bearing down on me beneath the quivering touch of that darkly snaking whip, a shiver racked my body. Suddenly the dark tomb seemed cold and eerie and I had the uncanny sensation that my father's presence, if it had been there at all, had fled, leaving me alone with my own terrifying thoughts.

"Father?" I called again in a softly quavering voice.

But it was no use. The magical spell had been shattered by the chilling thoughts of intrigue and death that crept across my mind and that revolved around an obsessive memory of dark eyes snapping at me like live coals out of dim shadows, reaching to compel me in an oddly frightening way that left me weak and shaken.

The dry chill of the vault seeped through me. Giving an involuntary little shudder, I held the lantern high to light my way through the gloom that had grown thick around me. Eagerly I sought the glimmer of moonlight that should have been there ahead of me, seeping in through the low, arched doorway.

But there was only a dense, smothering darkness beyond the pale circle of light cast by my flickering lantern. Even as I spun about in panic, fancying that I had somehow lost my way, the chilling grate of metal scraping against metal assaulted my eardrums as someone viciously crashed the thick bolt that sealed the vault's heavy doors.

Staying where I was for a spellbound moment or two, I fought down fear, telling myself that whoever was there had gone for a walk in the cemetery as I had done, and finding the doors to the tomb standing open, had decided to close them, unaware that someone was inside.

But what of the stones I had dragged into place to make certain that the thick, iron plates did not swing shut of their own accord, trapping me inside? Whoever was there would have had to remove those heavy pieces of rough rock and in so doing must surely have realized that they had been placed there for a reason.

It was then that I screamed, the shrill sound of my voice fading abruptly into dark oblivion. Rushing forward, the lantern dangling recklessly from fingers that had turned suddenly to ice, I pounded on the unresisting metal, commanding whoever was there beyond the solidly riveted panels to release me.

But it was no use. Whoever had been there was gone and I was alone, locked inside my father's tomb.

Chapter TEN

I turned frantically about, the glittering stones seeming to mock me with their tiny, shimmering shards of light. An eerie silence had invaded the crypt. The silence of death. . . . If my father's spirit had returned to comfort me, as I had wanted to believe earlier, it was no longer present. I was alone, shut securely behind the impenetrable iron doors by someone who must have been spying on me from some secretive hiding place of his own.

Who had watched me leave the mansion to climb the barren, moon-silvered slope between ghostly ranks of gray headstones, to enter my father's tomb? Greg Gallagher? Had he stationed himself behind the shuttered windows of the queerly shaped cupola that sat astride the roof of his darkened house and which seemed to nurture some virulent secret that would not bear up in the light of day? What had he in store for me now? Did he imagine that I would die of fear, locked inside the cold, dark tomb, or that I would perhaps starve to death, in time? Or had he some other plan in mind for me? For surely a search would be made, when Isabel and the Steps found that I was missing from my room. Would they think then to look for me in the vault?

Meanwhile, I was trapped. Going again to the heavy doors, I put down the lantern and pounded against them with doubled fists, calling as loudly as I could for help.

But it was no use. The sound of my voice was diminished almost at once by the earthen walls that surrounded me. The chances of it carrying beyond the solidly set doors seemed almost nonexistent when I stopped to consider that the mansion was situated at least a hundred yards down the slope. Exhausted by my efforts, I picked up the lantern and went again to my father's casket.

"Please," I whispered. "Please help me."

Pressing my forehead against the cold glass, I repeated his name over and over again in that same despairing voice. "Father? Father?"

A breath of cold air brushed over me, immediately raising the hackles on my neck. Someone . . . something had entered the tomb, dispelling the quiet of the dead. I sensed, rather than saw, that other invading presence that had destroyed the sensation of utter emptiness that had descended on me.

Turning swiftly about, I held the lantern high in an effort to illuminate the farthest reaches of the seemingly endless vault. My first thought was that someone had thrown wide the iron doors to admit a cool blast of evening air. But there was no welcoming spill of moonlight from that quarter, only a black wall of darkness to show me that the doors were still intact.

Whirling around, I called in a loud voice, "Who is it? Who's there?"

There was a subtle movement deep in the vault. Bats,

stirring to life because of the pale gleam of light from my lantern? Swinging the lantern protectively before me, I went on shaking legs in the direction of that dimly fleeting shadow.

"Father?" My voice quivered, betraying my fear. Swallowing the thickness that filled my throat, I asked again, "Father?"

"Not your father." The strained whisper that came to me out of those darkly eerie depths was so scarcely audible that at first I imagined my mind had begun to play tricks on me.

Nevertheless, I heard myself answering, as if whoever . . . whatever was there comprised a living, breathing entity. "Who then?" I commanded in that same shaking whisper. "Who are you if not my father?"

"Not your father," that same faint voice repeated. "Go away! Go away!"

But it was as if the blackly moving shadows deep in the vault had mesmerized me and I continued to advance toward the vague form that I was certain I saw there, outlined faintly against stones that shone gray in the pale glow from my lantern. Gradually, as I continued to move slowly forward, the uncertain shadow began to take shape and I was able then to make out the unmistakable form of a black-clad woman.

"Isabel?" I asked in a stunned voice. "What in heaven's name . . . ?"

But even before I could finish speaking, she was gone and there was no one there at all, the cavernous depths of the crypt looming suddenly ahead of me like a hungry, black mouth.

Was I going mad? Had the blow I'd received when I fell before the onslaught of Greg Gallagher's racing team addled my senses? For a moment or two I continued to stare ahead of me into that blackly yawning hole. But if Isabel had been there, she was gone and I was alone.

Turning back the way I had come, I went to fling myself against the vault's thick doors. Royce's offhand remark about a ghost pried chillingly at my befuddled thoughts.

"You can't deny that she's been seen since the accident," Emma had said of Loryea Labree. But if it had been Loryea Labree's ghost I had seen, why should she have

chosen to haunt my father's tomb? Was it because they had both died tragically? Was that the link that had drawn to my father's final resting place the spectral shadow of the woman I had glimpsed in the depths of the vault? As I huddled against the heavy doors I tried not to think that Greg Gallagher's name had been mentioned in connection with both of their deaths.

It seemed like an eon that I waited, beset by an unnerving host of chimerical questions that haunted my stunned thoughts, the night chill seeping in through the thick iron to numb my hands and feet. There seemed to be no way to escape the trap I had walked into. I could only wait and hope that I would be missed soon and a search party organized to comb the rugged gulches that scored the steep slopes of Sun Mountain in an attempt to discover where I had gone.

Or would Isabel and the Steps prefer to ignore the fact that I was missing until it was too late? Had it been one of them who'd followed me up the mountain to seal me inside the tomb in a determined effort to be rid of my burdensome presence? It would not bear thinking about.

Pushing the uneasy doubts aside, I lowered the lantern's dancing flame to conserve the dwindling supply of oil, and settled down as comfortably as I could to keep my anxious vigil.

The creeping cold must have caused me to drowse, for I awoke with a start, fancying that I had heard a sharp, rattling sound accompanied by a softly calling voice.

"Ol' woodpecker, he rap on the house when someone gonna die," Cleo, the young slave girl who had been more a companion than a maid to Melissa and me, opined out of the depths of my memory.

For a stunned moment or two, I imagined that I was back home, in Savannah, safe in the small, back bedroom that had been Melissa's nursery, lying tensely awake while I listened to the sudden whine of the hurricane winds that came sweeping wildly around the corners of the big house to set the stiff limbs of the big live oak outside my window tapping wildly against the white-painted balustrades of the upstairs veranda. I had known that the harsh rapping sounds came from the winds, in spite of Cleo's insistence that they heralded a sudden death in the family.

I shuddered, wondering if it had been Cleo's voice that awakened me, coming to me out of a past that was lost to me forever.

The thought had no sooner crossed my mind than I heard it again: the sudden, harsh rattle of the heavy bar that sealed the doors to the tomb. Someone was outside, trying to get in. Scrambling to my feet, I pressed my face close to the seam between the heavy, metal panels. But before I could make my presence known, a voice called out suddenly, "Loryea! For God's sake, come back!"

I stayed where I was, paralyzed by a cold wave of fear, for the voice I heard belonged to Greg Gallagher.

"Loryea!" His voice faded briefly, then grew louder as he came back to the doors of the tomb, calling her name again. "Loryea!"

There was the sudden, screeching sound of metal scraping against metal. Trembling, I snatched up the lantern. The quick motion caused the feeble flame to flicker wildly. Then, abruptly, it went out, plunging me into a bottomless well of darkness. Running blindly, I made my way deeper into the tomb.

But I was too late. The doors swung wide and he saw me.

Chapter ELEVEN

"Loryea." He came slowly toward me, his tall form silhouetted against the silvery moonlight that had washed all color from the world outside.

I cowered away from him.

"Loryea," he said again, hesitating briefly before taking another anxious step toward me.

He seemed oddly unreal, outlined against the tomb's

cavernous opening, the templelike monument casting its own black shadows beyond the open doors behind him. I wondered numbly if he'd been overcome by some strange form of madness. Were we both caught up in some monstrous nightmare that had addled our senses? Did that account for his not knowing who I was? Was that why he had called me by a dead woman's name?

"Put yo' hand on the head of a dead person, if you don' want her to worry you no more, or to haunt you," Cleo's voice whispered in the depths of my memory. "You never be afraid of death ever again, you do that. Jus' touch yo' hand to the top of her head, light like." The three of us, Melissa, Cleo and me, had slipped into the darkened front parlor where my mother's casket stood, her white face looking oddly waxen against the purple velvet lining.

Was that what had brought Greg to the cemetery? I wondered crazily. To touch the top of Loryea's head so that she would cease to haunt him? And what of my dead father? Was Greg Gallagher haunted by his own torturous intrigues that, if Isabel and the Steps were to be believed, had resulted in murder?

I had begun to tremble. Picking up my skirts in nervous fingers, I went by him, flying on numbed feet through the tomb's arched opening. Glancing over my shoulder, I saw him lunge out of the black shadows to come plunging after me, his booted feet sending up hollow echoes of sound as he swayed as gracefully as a cat between the darkly thrusting headstones.

"Julie!" Surprise edged his harshly commanding voice. "Wait! I want to speak to you."

Ignoring his summons, I swerved to avoid a mound of freshly turned earth, hearing him close behind me, his boots crunching across the ragged stones that were scattered across the billowing mountainside as if they had been flung carelessly aside by a giant hand. One of the stones rattled beneath the sole of my shoe, twisting my ankle, sending me flying headlong into a prickly clump of sage that suddenly loomed in my path.

In the next instant he was onto me, swooping to lift me in arms that fastened like steel bands around my panting body. The gravel had torn my hand when I'd fallen, ripping through the thin material of my petticoat to sear the skin from my knees.

"Oh my God, Julie!" He breathed into my hair, pressing my trembling form against his hard body that vibrated beneath the steady pumping of his heart.

Or was it my own fiercely throbbing heart I felt, jarring through us both so that I had the sudden wild sensation that we had, in that swiftly flashing moment, become as one? Breathlessly I clung to him, my aching lungs threatening to burst. The wounds on my hands and knees burned deplorably. I felt bruised and battered. Defeated by this strange, dark man who seemed so intent on destroying me for his own unfathomable reasons.

He spoke my name softly. I fancied I caught an underlying note of sorrow in his voice. As if, I thought, he regretted what he must do to me, but must do it nevertheless. Looking into his face, I made out the fiery glitter of his eyes. They burned down at me as they had done that first time, when I'd caught him watching me out of the shadows beneath the gallery that overhung the town's main street.

"Why?" I whispered. "Why must you do this to me? Why must you misuse me so abominably?"

"If this is misusing you, then I can't find it within myself to be sorry," he said, his arms refusing to yield their hold on me when I pushed against him. "It was my intention to save you from yourself. But since you seem to imagine I've failed you, I may as well compound the crime by taking full advantage of the situation."

He kissed me then, unmindful of the dust that had billowed up to coat my face when I fell and that seared my lips like an abrasive powder beneath the crushing force of his mouth. Briefly I fought against him. Then, as an oddly exciting warmth welled up in me, arousing in me a peculiarly languid feeling that seemed to turn my bones to water, I felt myself melting shamelessly against him, overwhelmed by that strangely seeping joy.

It was not until after we had torn apart that I remembered he had tried to kill me. A fury that drove all thought of danger from my mind possessed me and I lashed out savagely, "It must be obvious to you by now that I'm not the woman you first imagined me to be. I'm not Loryea Labree!"

He tensed, as if to spring. "What do you know of her?" he challenged. "Who told you about Loryea?"

I flinched away from him without answering, reaching to gather up my tattered skirts. But he was too fast for me. His hand darted out to grasp my arm, spinning me roughly about to face him.

"Tell me!" he commanded ruthlessly.

"I heard you calling her name," I said.

"Her first name only," he retorted.

"You must be mad!" I shot back at him, that same innate savagery that had prompted me to defy him earlier making me reckless now.

"Was it one of them? Marcus or Royce, perhaps? Or even Isabel?" he persisted, his words overridden by a strange urgency.

"They discussed her over dinner," I relented cautiously, something in his manner alerting me.

"What did they say?" he demanded. "What deceitful stories have they told you?"

"Nothing that I am not now prepared to believe," I said.

"Loryea is dead," he said, becoming oddly subdued. "Why can't they let her rest in peace?"

"Perhaps because of the kind of woman she was, she has obsessed you all," I said.

"Who are you to criticize Loryea?" he shot back angrily. "You can't possibly know the kind of person she was. They've lived too long with their twisted prejudices, in that house. That's what comes of having suddenly acquired a vast amount of wealth. Isabel and the rest of them were never equipped to handle it."

"Does that include my father?" I asked defensively.

"I liked your father," he said.

"Apparently you liked the mine better," I said recklessly. "Enough that you were ready to commit murder to have it."

Even in that peculiar half-light, I saw that I had goaded him too far. His face paled, his dark eyes glittering at me out of the stark shadows that ridged his sharply defined features, making his face seem suddenly masklike and decidedly evil. It was easy enough then for me to fancy that I saw treachery clearly written across the bold line of his mouth.

I tried to wrench away from him. But he kept me where I was, his voice barely discernible when he finally spoke, overridden as it was by that same strangely brooding melancholy which had seemed to suggest that he regretted what he must do to me but had no other choice left. "My God! Don't tell me they have accused me openly behind my back? As if I'd have wanted to harm a hair on his head. . . ." His voice dwindled away, weighted by that same leaden note of regret and I found myself thinking what a superb actor he was.

As determined as I was not to be taken in by his mercurial moods, I could not stop myself from asking then, "You knew my father well?" driven by a fundamental need to learn all I could about the man I had not seen since I was a child, but whom I had, nevertheless, continued to revere as the only father I had ever known.

"Well enough to have acquired a deeply abiding respect for him," Greg said almost kindly.

"You must have known, then, that the mine was no longer productive," I said. "Surely he had told you that himself, if the two of you were friends, as you claim."

"I knew," he said grimly. "Nor was it the first of the major shafts to go dry. But there's always the chance that a new ore body will turn up on another level."

"Apparently you were willing, if not eager, to take that chance," I said coldly.

"Surely Isabel hasn't neglected to tell you that the McKay-Ritchie adjoins my own claim," he retorted mockingly.

"And why not?" I shot back at him, not because I felt any particular loyalty to Isabel in spite of the fact that she was my stepmother, but because he had challenged me in a way that raised my ire. "Particularly since half of the mine belonged to her."

"And what of your own interest in the McKay-Ritchie, Miss McKay?" he demanded. "Your father was a fair-minded man. He can't have neglected to provide for you."

A small, cold, warning sensation darted along my spine when I remembered the legacy my father had mentioned to me in his letter. Had Greg taken the letter, after all, just as I had first suspected? Did that explain his reference now to my father's fair-mindedness in providing for me?

I stared up at him, attempting to read his face more clearly. But his expression was lost to me in that faint, clear light that cast its long, bleak shadows across the face of the mountain. He seemed suddenly to tower over me, mysterious, formidable, his mouth, which had only moments before turned my own lips to flame, smiling grimly.

Suddenly I was afraid. Seizing my chance, I jerked away from him and ran as fast as I could back to my father's house.

Alone in the comparative safety of my room, I huddled before the bay windows, half-expecting him to come bounding after me up the back stairs where Gertie had left a lamp burning, as she always did in the event that Royce would come stumbling home from his nightly carousal at a late hour. The thick, iron restraining chains that secured the house to the mountain were visible at either side of my window. Greg's house loomed bleakly beyond the taut chains, its grim facade visible through the delicately lacy leaves of the young trees that separated Isabel's garden from the yard terraced below the stone retaining wall that set the two houses apart and that was draped, miraculously, with rampant fronds of ivy. I had seen Sam shuffling along, yoked beneath buckets of water, to drench the young trees and thick vines, even though the town's water supply was nothing short of precarious. There would be plenty of water in time, when the pipeline that was being laid in the form of an inverted siphon from the towering, snow-clad Sierra to the west was completed, Isabel had said. Meanwhile, she would have her garden. All respectable residences had their garden, she'd told me, her chin lifting proudly.

A breeze had risen, dancing through the close rows of lilac bushes and the roses that Isabel was so proud of, causing the deep shadows to move eerily through the large garden. Was Greg there, crouching low behind one of the fragrant bushes, watching, as I was? Or had he dared, after all, to follow me into the house? I turned toward the door, listening.

But there were no stealthy creaks and groanings to

warn me of his approach and I turned back toward the darkened glass beyond the lace curtains, hearing only the far-off wail of coyotes baying mournfully at the moon.

Then, suddenly, I was alerted by the thudding pace of an approaching horse. Pressing my forehead against the cool glass, I strained to see the street, making out a solitary figure seated listlessly on a dark mount, his head and shoulders visible above the stone retaining wall that thrust up from the narrow track which passed before the two houses. Even though I could not see him clearly, I knew by the way he sat his horse that it was Dr. Thomas Quinn making his way along the drive that banked steeply upward between thick wings of stone, toward the carriage house and stable built into the hillside at the rear of Greg's mansion.

I watched him dismount, making out the glint of moonlight reflected in the small, oval lenses of his spectacles.

A darkly solitary figure strode down from the sharply rising knoll behind the carriage house to join him. Greg. The two of them then went together into the darkened stable, emerging a moment or two later to enter the tightly shuttered house below.

I stayed where I was behind the lace panels, mesmerized by an oddly virulent curiosity. Had Greg's housekeeper, Bertha Foster, been taken ill? Did that explain Dr. Quinn's late arrival? And what of those other times when I had watched him dismount before Greg's house to stumble up to the front door, where he disappeared from view, lost to me in the bleak shadows? What drew him so frequently to the darkly shuttered house next door?

There seemed to be no feasible explanation for his presence there and, telling myself that it was really none of my concern as long as it did not involve me, I started to turn away. As I did so I was arrested by a peculiar glimmer of light sparkling against the darkly shuttered windows of the cupola that thrust up from the roof of Greg's house. At first I imagined that it had been caused by some trick of the moonlight. Then I saw that it was not a reflection after all, but a faint rim of light burning behind the tightly closed shutters. Even as I continued to watch, that thin sliver of light was quickly stifled, as if whoever was there had reached to draw a thick curtain into place behind the blackened panes, and I could not help thinking that whoever was there wanted to make certain that his presence in the oddly shaped tower room would not be betrayed.

I had the eerie sensation that someone watched the windows of my own room from behind those tightly guarded panes and I moved hastily away from the thin curtains, reaching behind them to draw the green roller shades before I dared to light my candle.

When I had laid out the new cambric nightdress Cleo had made for me in preparation for my journey west, I blew out the tiny flame, sliding out of my clothes in the security of darkness, my finely honed instincts telling me that there was some connecting thread woven stealthily through the events and scandals that surrounded the two houses. If only I could grasp it, I thought, I should be able then to unravel the secrets behind my father's death and his missing letter.

Chapter TWELVE

Emma appeared, hollow-eyed, at breakfast, the others having remained in their beds, as was their habit. It had not taken me long to discover that Isabel and the Steps held to no regular schedule, as had been the case in Uncle Grant's household, back home in Savannah. There, no one had been exempt from his duties, following the devastating effects of the war, with the exception, perhaps, of Melissa, who had been permitted the dubious luxury of becoming a slug-a-bed.

"You're limping," Emma observed when I entered the dining room, her tone oddly accusing.

Her gaze had fastened itself on my face in a way which seemed to suggest that she hoped to ferret out some particularly odious bit of incriminating evidence that could be used against me.

"I went for a walk late last night," I said, watching her closely for a reaction. "On my way back I stumbled on a stone and fell."

"On your way back from *where?*" Emma demanded.

"I went to my father's tomb," I said, undaunted by her fierce glare.

It seemed to me then that her face suddenly paled. Or did I only imagine that the color drained from her already colorless features because of the room's poor lighting? I was able to convince myself that something like that had been the case when she said, in her coldly indifferent voice, "Perhaps you should be more careful where you go off to after this."

But I did not miss the gleam of curiosity behind her grape-green eyes that turned them oddly feverish, as if she suspected me of attempting to hide something from her. I decided then that, for all of her remote indifference, she was far more perceptive than I had at first been willing to give her credit for being.

I was certain of it when she went on, in that same accusing way, "It seems a foolish thing to go wandering around up there between the headstones at night when heaven only knows whom one might accidentally encounter. It's not as if I were merely being superstitious, you know. It's common knowledge here that Loryea's spirit has failed to find rest the way most mortals do after they've departed this life. And small wonder, considering the kind of life she led while she lived." Emma's look had turned calculating and I guessed that she was attempting to assess just how far she could go with me and still hope to be believed. "She's come to be known locally as the woman in black," she said then. She paused, her pale eyes gleaming more brightly than ever. "I've seen her ghost more than once, wandering around up there between the markers."

Feigning an indifference that I was far from feeling, I went on shaky legs to the sideboard. Lifting the warming cover from the hot platter Gertie had left there, I speared fragrant slices of ham onto my plate.

When I could trust myself to speak, I said, "There's

some reason why she wears black, I suppose," my voice, which was as coolly remote as Emma's had been, sounding slightly foreign even to my own ears, for inside my chest my heart thudded wildly as I recalled my own chilling encounter with the woman in black.

Who had she been? I was not so ingenuous as to let myself be taken in by Emma's strange tale of a ghost who roamed at night between the headstones that dotted the rugged flanks of Sun Mountain. Yet I could not deny that there had been someone there in the vault with me. Whoever it was had wanted me to go away. Why? Why had that darkly clad form ordered me to depart? Had she been trying, in her own horrifying way, to warn me?

"She was slightly demented, even while she lived," Emma was saying, as calmly as if we had been discussing a mutual friend who'd moved away and left us. "Her activities were never what you might refer to as 'normal.' "

After pouring coffee for myself and returning to my place at the big table, I said, "Are you telling me she was mad?"

"What would *you* say of a woman who dared to appear in a scandalously revealing pair of pink tights?" Emma demanded with a show of spirit.

I stared incredulously into her plain features, which had turned slightly smug.

"She was no better than the trollops who live on sporting row," she went on, her voice edged with disfavor. "Her kind always wields a certain power over men, vile creatures that they can sometimes be. That's why it is so vitally important for women like Mother and myself to strive to maintain a certain position in this terrible place. There are far too few who are willing to speak out openly against the element Loryea had come to represent."

"You make her sound quite wicked," I said weakly, not at all certain what kind of woman Loryea had been.

Had she, like the notoriously famous Julia Bulette, held court for her many admirers in that section of town that respectable women dared to speak of only in whispers? More scandalously still, had she done so clad only in a scanty pair of pink tights, as Emma had suggested? The fact that Greg Gallagher had been among her admirers, according to what had been said over dinner the previous evening, only served to increase my dismay, for I had not imagined him to be the kind of man who must frequent houses of ill repute in order to satisfy his more brutal cravings.

"Loryea was far from being an angel, I assure you," Emma said.

"Did I hear poor Loryea's name mentioned?" Royce's voice said from the doorway.

I turned to find him watching us, clad in the fur-trimmed dressing gown that he had worn the first time I'd seen him.

"I was telling Julie what a scandal she made of herself," Emma said primly. "Every libertine in town was panting after her, following her indecent display, including, I'm ashamed to say, my own two brothers. You can imagine how poor Mother and I felt. There wasn't a woman in the audience at Piper's Opera House that night whose face didn't burn with shame for the brazen creature. She might just as well have presented herself to us in a state of total dishabille."

"I daresay it wouldn't have been nearly so titillating as the pink tights she wore," Royce commented, flashing me one of his wicked little smiles. "The opera house all but shifted on its foundations, as every man in the place leaned forward in his seat to better assess her comely attributes."

"Royce! You are even more vile than I have given you credit for being," Emma snapped.

"I should consider myself a most unfortunate specimen if it were otherwise," Royce retorted.

"She was an actress, then," I said.

"One of the best," Royce told me. "She attracted a great deal of attention with her dramatic portrayals. Few of her contemporaries had her knack for originality. The night she appeared as Mazeppa, clad in her pink tights, she had the imagination to come flashing onto the stage astride a handsome white steed. I daresay it was a first in theatrical history."

"And a last, I should hope," Emma complained.

Royce, if he had heard, preferred to ignore her, enthusing to me over the new opera house that had a steel-spring-supported floor, a stage that sloped toward the audience, and was an incredible fifty feet deep and thirty feet wide.

"Loryea wasn't the only beauty to grace those boards," he said. "Theatergoers here have been enthralled by such well-known personages as Lily Langtry, Lotta Crabtree, and Lola Montez, who has since become a legend in her own time. Loryea's ingenious interpretations would have taken her equally far had she had the good fortune to live."

. . . the good fortune to live. Icy fingers touched my spine, sending an involuntary little shudder through me. What cruel Fate had determined that it was Loryea's time to die? Or had Fate had nothing to do with it at all? Had someone taken it upon himself to intervene in her life, just as I was convinced Greg Gallagher had tried to do when he had sent his team thundering down on me?

I brushed the chilling thoughts aside, picking up the thread of Emma's monologue that had taken on the unmistakably righteous overtones of a tirade. ". . . and had she not seen fit to lower herself to become a detestation to respectable women," she was saying senselessly, her tone echoing Isabel's obsession with what she constantly referred to as the "refinements." "She seemed determined to seduce every man who crossed her path."

"Her admirers loved nothing better than showering her with bullion and jewels," Royce said in his taunting way. "Being an actress, she knew how to make herself exciting. Stage people are notoriously witty."

"Not all of them," Emma shot back at him, their gazes locking briefly in some secret contretemps of their own.

"I've never had the pleasure of knowing anyone who chose the stage as a way of life," I said.

"And just as well," Emma said. "It was inevitable that Loryea should die a dramatic death. Her kind usually does."

"You needn't sound so smugly self-righteous about it, Emma," Royce said, going to serve himself from the generously appointed sideboard.

"How *did* she die?" I could not refrain from asking, in spite of the reluctance Royce had displayed over dinner the night before when the subject of Loryea's death had been brought up. "A particularly heinous murder," he had said then, in voicing his protest.

"She was scalded with acid," Emma said quickly, as if she were determined to cut short any further protest Royce might feel compelled to make. "Her face was completely destroyed."

"How horrible!" I gasped, visualizing with jarring clarity the shadowy form that had accosted me from the depths of the vault.

For the first time it occurred to me that the darkly ethereal ghost-woman I had seen hovering just beyond the reach of my light had hidden her face behind a veil. Had it been because she had no face to hide?

But there was no such thing as a ghost, I quickly reminded myself, in spite of Cleo's numerous references to haunts that must constantly be pacified and, now, Emma's apparent determination to convince me that Loryea's spirit could not rest because of the indiscretions she had committed while she lived. If there had indeed been someone in the vault besides myself, it had been a living, breathing entity.

Who then? Who had disguised himself, or herself, as a dead woman to slip by me, unnoticed, into the cavernous crypt? Was it a real woman who had flung those veiled warnings at me? Emma, perhaps? Was she even more clever than I wanted to believe, behind her unimaginative—and odiously self-righteous—facade? Did that explain her determination to make me believe she had actually seen the woman in black wandering about the cemetery on those other occasions?

"She always prized her looks, being an actress," Emma was saying.

"All the more reason to suspect that whoever flung acid into her face was determined to destroy her beauty," Royce said, seating himself beside me with a little grimace.

"It sounds almost spiteful," I said. "As if whoever did it wanted to destroy her looks for other men. Perhaps he hadn't intended for her to die, at all."

"There is the availability of the acid to be considered, too, of course," Royce said in a tone which seemed to indicate that if I was to be told the whole story, it was best to get it finished with as prudently as possible. "The

. . . accident took place in the vicinity of one of the mine assay offices, which somewhat narrows down the field of suspicion."

"Julie is bound to find out sooner or later, if she stays on here any time at all, that it happened at Greg Gallagher's place of business," Emma said.

I think I had known, even before she spoke, that Greg had been somehow involved.

"He used oil of vitriol," Royce went on doggedly. "Ordinarily, it isn't of a strength to burn very deeply. But whoever did it used the pure solution, which seemed to suggest that he was either entirely ignorant of the acid's properties or that he fully intended to destroy her. Needless to say, it was necessary to seal the casket Greg bought for her. A pity, too, since it was the best money could buy. The color of the lining would have become her."

"I thought you had no taste for the macabre," Emma remarked.

"I was fond of Loryea, as you well know," Royce said. "It pleases me to think that Greg chose her coffin with some consideration for her own personal tastes."

"It was certainly no secret to me, or anyone else in town, that you were seeing her, along with the rest of them," Emma said with asperity. "Although I won't go so far as to suggest that it was you who had become her benefactor. Whoever he was, he must have strongly resented the attention she squandered on her many admirers. As I recall, Tom Quinn had become a particular favorite of hers." Emma's tone was scornful and openly taunting.

"It would appear to me that Greg Gallagher had become her benefactor," I forced myself to observe. "Why else should he have felt obligated to provide a casket for her . . . remains?" I shivered again, pushing aside my plate.

"No doubt he was attempting to absolve himself," Royce said obscurely. "Loryea had a twin sister who died a couple of years ago, under mysterious circumstances that were never satisfactorily explained. Greg was betrothed to her, at the time. Her name was Laura, by the way. She and Loryea were identical in every respect, aside from their temperaments, which were as different as night from day. Laura was the quiet one, ideally suited to becoming the wife of an up-and-coming nabob."

"I had no idea that you were so observing," Emma remarked, regarding Royce with suspicion.

Royce shrugged. "I only know what I've heard. There are those who believe Greg feels driven to invest all of his energy in the mines, as a means of escape from the guilts that beset him. Maybe he hopes to make it up to himself for both of their deaths by adding to his already considerable store of wealth, hand over fist. Whatever his reasons, Loryea's continued presence here, after Laura died, must have been a painful reminder to him. He couldn't have helped seeing Laura every time he looked at her. Not that he would ever have admitted as much. He's far too clever to give himself away."

I looked curiously at Royce, alerted by his intuitive observations which seemed to suggest a side to his nature I had not yet seen. Was he the one who was being clever, by casting his veiled aspersions at Greg? What passions raced unheeded behind my handsome stepbrother's wickedly jocular demeanor? Was his libertine pose merely a cover-up for a deeper, more sensitive nature that he felt compelled, for reasons of his own, to hide.

I thought how little I really knew about any of them. Least of all, Greg Gallagher, who had apparently had sufficient reasons of his own for wanting to rid himself of Loryea's haunting presence. Obviously he had not succeeded, for I could not forget that he had mistaken me for Loryea's ghost when he'd come upon me in my father's vault.

Beside me, Royce said, "I have to run now. Stay and finish your coffee with poor Emma, Julie. She can use some moral support."

"And what, exactly, is that supposed to mean?" Emma demanded.

"I saw Renny lose at cards last night, and not for the first time." Royce gave a careless shrug.

"My husband's luck at cards is none of your concern," Emma snapped.

"It is when it falls on poor Mother's shoulders to pay off his debts," Royce said.

"And what of your own losses?" Emma flung back at him.

But he had already gone, flashing me a last quick smile across the fur collar of his dressing gown as he went out through the door. A moment or two later I heard him running up the stairs, the sound of his footsteps muffled by the red plush runner.

"My brother is a decidedly wicked man," Emma snorted when the sound of his steps had faded.

"Men have certain needs," I said abstrusely, quoting Aunt Hillary.

"How delicately you put it, Julie," Emma quipped, apparently more determined than ever to take her ill temper with Royce out on me. "One would almost be led to suspect that you are rather well informed in such matters. Like Loryea," she added spitefully, as if she had seen into my mind and knew that I was perversely fascinated with the tragic tale she and Royce had pieced together.

"I was reared in an atmosphere which makes it easy for me to accept life's grosser realities," I countered coolly, in an effort to disguise what amounted to a growing preoccupation with Greg Gallagher and his motives.

"Am I to assume that you won't mind a great deal if, when you finally marry, your husband chooses to associate with women like Loryea Labree during his spare hours?"

"I should try to remedy such a situation, of course," I said. "I should never permit my own sense of respectability to stand in the way of my domestic happiness."

"You sound very sure of yourself," Emma said scathingly. "Almost as if you have someone in mind whom you intend to try to make over."

"Don't be preposterous," I shot back at her. "How could I possibly when I have only just recently arrived here."

"I haven't missed the way Royce watches you," Emma said craftily.

And your own precious Renny, I wanted to retort, suddenly despising her hateful vindictiveness.

Instead, I said, more agitated by her clever observations than I wanted to be, "I'm not taken in by the looks Royce gives me. It would be utterly absurd for me even to consider his gallantry in any serious vein. I'm certain that all he intends to do is tease me a little. As does Renny," I could not resist adding. "It would be a mistake for any woman to take their amusing sallies too seriously. Now, if you'll please excuse me, I have business to attend to in town today. I want to catch Sam before he leaves with the carriage to drive Gertie to do her marketing."

Folding my napkin carefully beside my plate, I whirled away from Emma's pale stare, running hurriedly up the stairs, as if by so doing I could escape the seething doubts that taunted me.

More determined than ever to call on my father's attorneys, I dressed carefully for the occasion, as befitted the heiress to whatever small fortune he may have seen fit to bequeath me, selecting a town dress in mauve-flowered brocade that Melissa had discarded two seasons before, after having worn it only once. The color, which had been all wrong for her, brought out the delicate peach tones of my skin and enhanced the coppery highlights in my hair, which I allowed to fall loosely onto my shoulders, securing its long tresses beneath the satin ribbon of my coal-scuttle bonnet.

I was not displeased with my appearance when I set out a few minutes later in search of Gertie, my bruised ankle all but forgotten in my eagerness to have my tumultuous affairs settled once and for all by persons in authority. Overwhelmed as I still was by the sudden revelation I had experienced inside my father's tomb, I refused even to consider the possibility that the members of the law firm which had, according to the few facts I'd been able to glean from Isabel, been in charge of my father's affairs prior to his death, might refuse to acknowledge me.

I found Gertie in her room behind the kitchen, preparing to join Sam, who had the carriage out and waiting.

"You barely touched your plate this morning, Miss Julie," the plump housekeeper scolded in motherly tones. "Are you sure, now, you've got strength enough left in you to go gallavantin' off?"

"I'd scarcely call it gallavanting, since it is my intention to call on my father's attorneys," I said.

"A fine man, your father." Gertie tossed a knitted shawl across her fleshy shoulders, leading the way out through the back door. "More's the pity he's dead now, poor soul, and him only just beginning to realize the fruits of his labors, as they say."

"Maybe, in a way, his death was a mercy, with the mine going dry," I said.

"That's one way of looking at it, I suppose," Gertie said. "Although there's always rumors floating around that one or another of the big mines is petering out. Gravy one day and beans the next is the natural way of things here. He would have recovered himself quick enough, since there's always more where the first come from in these raw hills. It's happened time and again that a mine has gone dry, only to come back again better than ever. It's that uncanny, the way the mines exert their own personalities on the men inside." She flashed me a brightly confiding look. "They don't call them 'she's' for nothing. It's the same as with ships. Mine, ships, and women." She chuckled gleefully at her own small jest. "There's not one of them that's not notoriously fickle. Mr. Gallagher counted on that when he took over the McKay-Ritchie from Mrs. McKay and the rest of them."

"I've heard all about Mr. Gallagher," I said.

"I doubt that," Gertie said. "Seein' that you have only their version of what he's like to go by," she added, darting me a sly look.

"You and Bertha Foster, next door, must be good friends," I commented, convinced that Gertie was the type who would not hesitate to exchange raunchy morsels of gossip with anyone who had the patience to listen.

"We get on well enough, I suppose, all things considered."

"I couldn't help noticing from the windows of my room that the doctor calls there often," I said.

"We all have our small complaints, and that's the truth." Gertie climbed after me into the waiting carriage. When she had settled herself firmly on the leather seat, she turned to give me a piercing look. "You're that curious about him, ain't you? Not that I can say I blame you. He's a fine-looking specimen of a man. Every gal in town who's looking to snare herself a rich husband has set her sights on Greg Gallagher at one time or another. There was even a time when Miss Emma had hopes in that direction. That was before her mama bought that no-good Eyetalian count for her, the same as she bought and paid for all them other worthless baubles that happened to catch Miss Emma's eye."

"You're forgetting that I'm a member of this family," I said hautily, my cheeks flaming beneath the penetrating stare she had turned on me.

Her blunt insights into my motives perturbed me more than I cared to admit, least of all to myself. For in spite of my efforts to put from my mind all thought of Greg Gallagher, his presence next door continued to haunt me in a way that made me uneasy. What would Gertie say if she were to guess that he had kissed me in that fiercely possessive way that had completely addled my wits, causing me to lose all sense of propriety? Would she scorn me for a foolish addlepate who had no better sense than to fall for a man who was in love with a dead woman?

"You're John McKay's daughter," she was saying, her voice cutting suddenly across my thoughts.

"How can you know that for certain?" I demanded, instantly alerted by her positive tone.

"Because you're the spittin' image of him, that's why," Gertie stated in that same positive way. "Maybe your hair and eyes are a different color than his was. But you've got that same stubborn tilt to your jaw. I'd know you for John McKay's gal anywhere."

"You're the first one to tell me that," I said, wanting to believe her, yet not quite certain that I could trust her.

"The others are too wrapped up in themselves to see beyond the ends of their noses. If you'll excuse me for saying so," she added, with a pertinent lift of her plump chin. "I knew John McKay in the old days, before he stumbled onto all of that gold and silver that has made Isabel so high and mighty. Mrs. McKay, that is. I knew them both through rough times and good."

She rattled on. But I was no longer listening. For it had occurred to me that, if Gertie had so readily seen a resemblance between me and my dead father, it was not impossible that Greg Gallagher also had been aware of a certain likeness. Which seemed suddenly to explain how he had come to know me that first day, when I had stepped off of the stage to go scurrying off along Virginia City's dusty streets in search of a livery.

In a town that ran rampant with gossip, it was not inconceivable to imagine that he had learned of my impending arrival from someone who was closely associated with the Wells Fargo Company office, where I had sent the telegram that had been intended for my father. It remained only for him to determine which of the passengers aboard the incoming stage was John McKay's daughter, a choice that had been resolved for him by my chance resemblance to my father.

Apparently he had experienced no difficulty in identifying me.

But why? Why had he taken it upon himself to watch for me? What cruel motives drove him in his determination to be rid of me?

Chapter THIRTEEN

The town seethed with activity, as it had the day of my arrival, the laden ore wagons that moved ponderously toward the booming stamp mills situated at the base of the hill raising horrendous clouds of dust that settled over me like powder.

I paused briefly to read the familiar name stamped on the sides of the green-painted freighters that carried tons of gray rock which had been blasted from several of the mine's deeper drifts and which, according to Tim, was considered by Greg to be worth the trouble to mill, in spite of its low grade.

The main shaft, however, had remained closed since the day my father had died.

Hurrying on, I pushed my way past the swinging doors of the rollicking saloons, coming at last to the stair that Gertie had told me would take me up to Mr. Gridley's offices, which were located above a bustling merchandising firm.

"There's two other barristers that share the space with him," Gertie had said when I'd climbed down from the carriage. "But be sure now to ask for Mr. Gridley. I happen to know he and your father were good friends."

Taking heart from her comforting words, I climbed between wainscoted walls to a dark landing that opened into a waiting room filled with ponderous oak furniture. A Boston fern thrived in a pot before dust-caked windows that looked down on the street. On the dingy panes of the windows the name of the firm was inscribed in gold leaf above a shining, brass cuspidor that was conveniently situated between two stiff-backed leather chairs. I had no sooner gained my bearings than a nearby door opened to reveal a tall, gray-haired man whose blue eyes twinkled curiously from behind steel-rimmed spectacles set precariously astride the bridge of his slightly bulbous nose.

"I'd like to see Mr. Gridley, please," I said.

"I'm Mr. Gridley, my dear. What can I do for you?" He wore mutton-chop whiskers that stood out in queer little puffs below his ears and a full moustache that all but hid his mouth. But I could not mistake the good humor I glimpsed in his eyes and that sent an unwarranted wave of hope surging through me.

"I'm Julie McKay," I said a little breathlessly. "I've come to speak to you concerning the legacy my father left me."

His smile faded. "John McKay's daughter?"

I nodded vigorously.

"My dear, I can't tell you how deeply sorrowful I was to learn of your father's tragic death." He reached to take my hand in a fatherly gesture. "Now what's this business about a legacy? I assume you've brought me some document to verify your claim?" He glanced expectantly at my reticule.

"But I came all this way from Savannah, fully expecting you to have the proper documents on file in your safe," I said.

"I don't relish telling you this, my dear. But this office has no such papers in its possession. Your father's estate was settled some time ago. Shortly after his death, as a matter of fact." I fancied that some of the good humor had left him, giving rise to a glimmer of suspicion, as if, like the others, he was reluctant to take me at my word.

"But how can that be?" I protested. "He told me himself in a letter I had from him shortly before he died that he fully intended to consult you concerning the legality of the papers in question. He wanted to make certain that they were in order. Not that I'm a greedy person," I quickly added. "But I am a young woman alone in the world, and although I am equipped, after a fashion, to look after myself, I can't afford to overlook the possibility that he intended to see me taken care of. Particularly since he had suggested it himself in the letter I just mentioned."

"I appreciate your position, Miss McKay," Mr. Gridley said in a kindly voice. "But that doesn't alter the situation. Your father failed to consult this office, if that was, indeed, his intention."

"Do you doubt my word, Mr. Gridley?" I demanded heatedly.

"I am merely saying that your father left no papers with me."

It seemed a pity that, despite my first generous impression of him, I distinctly sensed his rejection of me.

"Could my father possibly have left with another attorney some evidence of whatever it was he had intended for me to have?" I asked rather desperately. "He didn't mention you by name in his letter, as I recall. Only that he had planned to get in touch with his agents the following morning to have the paper he had told me about witnessed and recorded by the proper authorities. 'To render it indisputable,' is the way he put it."

"That would seem to indicate that it was his intention for you to have a piece of his property," Mr. Gridley conceded. "A share in a mining claim, perhaps. But I happen to know that he owned no other property, apart from those assets which he bequeathed to Isabel."

I stared up at him in abject silence, striving desperately to find an excuse for my father's negligence. Why had he bothered to write to me at all if he had had no real intention of making good his promises? What had happened to cause him to so promptly forget about me?

"It might be of some help if you were to show me this letter you mentioned," Mr. Gridley said.

"I . . . I no longer have it," I admitted regretfully.

"I'm sorry, Miss McKay. I would like to be able to help you. But under the circumstances. . . ." He smiled ruefully. "After all, John has been gone now for over a year. If there had been any papers that were overlooked at the time of his death, surely someone would have uncovered them before this."

"I've been told he was murdered," I said. "Which seems to suggest to me that someone may have stolen them."

"There was no proof of that. And even if it were true, what could the murderer have hoped to gain? Sooner or later the papers would have had to come to light, particularly if they had involved a recorded mining property."

"Surely there were others here, besides my stepmother, who believed something like that may have been possible."

"Rumors of foul play are not uncommon here."

"Is nothing ever done to follow them up?" I asked.

"When there is sufficient evidene to warrant it. Your father's death was, quite plainly, accidental. Greg Gallagher testified to that. He had gone out for an early-morning ride and saw someone stirring near the mine. By the time he reached it, your father was gone. Greg went for help to bring him out. Tim. Marcus. Royce. All of them had a hand in helping him to recover the body."

"But it was Greg who found him," I said.

Mr. Gridley nodded his shaggy head.

Just as it was Greg who tried to run me down, I could not stop myself from thinking, feeling that same chilling sense of disaster that had gripped me then washing through me in a cold wave.

"They were alike, your father and Greg Gallagher. Both of them were in the habit of going up to check on the mines at odd hours. It was purely by chance that Greg had ridden out early that morning of June twelfth. It's a date that will be forever imprinted on my memory, out of respect for a good man."

June twelfth. The date at the top of my father's letter had been June eleventh. He had penned the message late in the evening, which meant that he had died during the early-morning hours of that same night. It seemed, suddenly, to be more than a shattering coincidence that he had taken it upon himself to let me know of my legacy shortly before he died.

"We learned later that someone had ridden up to the house to warn him that a fire had started in the mine," Mr. Gridley was saying in a tone that, like his face, was suddenly expressionless. "No one knows for certain who it was that carried that frightening message to John. He was a restless sleeper, given to pacing the floors and riding out to check on his workers at all hours. For that reason, he and Isabel had separate rooms. Whoever had warned him had come and gone before he woke her to tell her what had happened. He wanted to make certain for himself that there was some truth in the rumor, before he alerted the fire fighters. You have to understand, Miss McKay, what a terrible thing a mine fire can be. It's enough to strike the fear of God into us all."

"Was there a fire?"

"No, thank God for that much. Whoever had ridden up the hill to warn him had been wrong. It was thought later that it had been someone on the relay shift that had knocked off at four o'clock that morning. Although no one came forward to admit it, out of a sense of guilt, perhaps. There was never anyone in the mine between four and seven A.M., when the day shift came on. He'd laid off the watchman when the main vein played out. Said it was an unnecessary expense, since there was no rich jewelry ore laying around for the high-graders to carry off."

"Apparently it could have been anyone in town who came to warn him, then," I said.

"Emma told us later she'd heard voices late that night outside her window," Mr. Gridley said. "But she was still half-asleep and wasn't able to tell us whose they were, other than to say that whoever had been talking to John had been a man."

She had not quite dared, then, to accuse Greg outright, I thought. Nevertheless, she must have told Isabel and the others that she suspected him. Why else should Isabel be so adamant in her belief that Greg Gallagher had killed my father?

"We've an unholy fear of fire in this town," Mr. Gridley

was saying. "It's possible that whoever warned your father actually believed that there was some danger. Maybe the fellow had caught a whiff of some Chinaman's laundry fire and imagined the smoke had drifted up out of the main shaft."

"I can't believe my father died because of some Chinaman's laundry fire," I said.

"Only those of us who've fought such a blaze can appreciate the terror a mine fire inspires in otherwise calm and sensible men," Mr. Gridley said earnestly. "Your father was a conscientious employer who spared himself no effort where the safety of his workers was concerned. He was the first of the mine owners to install underground infirmaries where men who had been overcome by heat could be taken for treatment. Hell itself hath no fury to compare to flames raging out of control eight hundred feet beneath the earth's surface. Literally thousands of lives are threatened every time a fire breaks out in one of the subterranean drifts or chambers. There's a labyrinth of timber underneath this town, Miss McKay. Fire has been known to smolder down there for as long as three years, in the sealed-off drifts that have become tombs for the men who were caught in a holocaust of exploding gases. Steam is sometimes forced into the deeper levels in an attempt to save lives. But all too often the men who are trapped down there are cooked alive in water brought to a boil by the raging flames. If I sound crass or cruel, Miss McKay, it is only because I hope to impress on you why your father felt impelled to go to the mine that night, on the basis of such scant evidence."

"Please don't try to convince me that my father died a hero," I said shortly, more horrified than I wanted to admit by the frightful conditions that existed beneath the precariously perched city. "At best, his death was a senseless accident. At worst, it may very well have been murder, just as Isabel said."

"I haven't failed to consider the possibility that there may have been a fire, after all, and your father had succeeded in extinguishing it before he died." Mr. Gridley said, his tone of voice gently reprimanding me.

"Whose side are you on, Mr. Gridley?" I shot back at him out of an unbearable sense of frustration.

"The side of justice, Miss McKay," he said. "We may never know the real truth of the matter, now that it's over and done with. But if there is ever any way I can be of service to you, please feel free to call on me at any time. John McKay was my friend, may he rest in peace."

His words rang through my troubled thoughts like a funeral dirge: *Over and done with. Rest in peace. Rest in peace.*

Chapter FOURTEEN

Over and done with. Rest in peace. Rest in peace. The drumming words sent a wave of dizziness through me and I hurried out into the early-morning sunlight that was heavily laden with dust motes, haunted by that same curious ambivalence that had possessed me inside the tomb—a fleeting intimacy with my father's spirit that had given way to that other coldly seeping presence that had appeared to be heavily veiled in the black garb of mourning.

Of one thing I was certain: There had been no peace there; no comforting sensation of a life neatly finished and done with, the ragged edges nicely tucked away, the final thread tied. The atmosphere inside the tomb had been oppressive, the shadows cast by the light from my lantern wandering restlessly along the stone walls like anxious wraiths who could find no rest.

Breathing deeply in an effort to clear my thoughts of those haunting presences that seemed suddenly to stalk me, I quickened my pace, scurrying past a noisy melodeon, the gaily tinkling music that spilled out through the open doors seeming suddenly to mock me. Brushing past a blind organ grinder who leaned listlessly against a nearby wall, bearing the weight of a consumptive monkey on a stick-thin shoulder, I reached automatically for my reticule.

Then, remembering that I had been left destitute by

whoever had stolen the letter which had contained all that I owned in the world, apart from the few pieces of baggage I'd brought with me, I hurried on, the weary little tune from the beggar's organ trailing faintly behind me.

Pausing briefly, I sought Gertie's rosy face in the midst of the seething activity that gave rise to a harsh cacophony of sounds on every side, blotting out the last dismal threads of the plaintive little tune. But there was no sign of either her or Sam, who had perched like a yellow gnome in the box of Isabel's carriage, behind a prancing team of white horses that he had groomed, on my stepmother's orders, to a silvery sheen.

Deciding on impulse to walk the short distance up the hill, I turned at the next corner, focusing my attention on the big house that strained at its thick chains as if to free itself of whatever grim secrets were hidden behind its darkly glaring windows. As had happened on that other occasion, when I had first seen it from the windows of the bouncing stagecoach, I fancied that someone watched from behind the blackly gleaming panes of the queer little room that thrust up from its hipped roof and I strained to see past their shimmering surfaces. But to no avail. If someone had been there against Isabel's orders—for I could not forget that she had castigated both Royce and Emma for their bad taste in going there—whoever it was had gone and there were only the shadows that lurked beyond the filaments of curtains that were faintly visible from that distance behind the shining sheets of glass.

Was it only a reflection I had seen, after all, catching at the polished panes, triggering my fancy because of the dark doubts that beset me? I wanted to believe that it was; that there was no danger lurking inside the big house, waiting to catch me off my guard. But I could not help noticing, as I began to climb past shabby board houses tucked in between the monstrous rubble piles from the mines, that my father's house cast its long, black shadow over the house below, the grimly falling umbra seeming somehow portentous.

It seemed even more significant that my father's house should be the one that loomed so threateningly, the evil I had sensed lurking behind the tower-room windows that first day seeming to spill out from it in a dark cloud, and

I continued to stare up the hill in an attempt to sort out the conflicting impressions the two houses had inspired in me. Where did the real threat lie? Behind the secretive facade of Greg Gallagher's tighly shuttered mansion? Or did the danger I sensed lurk nearer at hand? Was it one of the Steps, or Isabel, perhaps, whose resentment I had come to feel so keenly? Which of them had masqueraded as Loryea Labree's ghost, slipping unseen into my father's tomb to confront me out of dim shadows that had safely concealed his or her identity? Why? Why must I go away? What was in the vault that whoever it had been had not wanted me to find?

My gaze went to the pale monument that guarded the vault's iron doors and for a fleeting instant I fancied that I saw a softly shifting movement beneath its shadowed overhang Then, just as quickly, that uneasy play of light and darkness vanished and there was only the ornate temple standing in isolated splendor against the face of the mountain that presented its own tumultuous contrasts, scored as it was by a vivid pattern of early-morning light and shadow, the sun gilding its tawny ridges above darkly slashing gullies.

I was distracted from my uneasy reverie by the sudden rattle of wheels approaching me from behind and I spun sharply around to see Marcus bearing down on me in a smartly polished phaeton, its top folded back to reveal his cleanly shining blondness. I was not unaware of the contrast he presented to Greg Gallagher's darkly handsome looks, thinking that, like the sharply patterned mountain, the two of them presented their own stark contrasts.

Like Marcus, the equipage he drove was polished to a high patina, catching my eye in spite of my determination not to be overly impressed by the lavish displays of wealth that were visible to me on every side, presenting yet another contrast between blatant opulence and the downtrodden appearance of those who had not been quite so successful in finding the fortunes they sought.

I had not been unaware that both Marcus and Royce owned their own private means of transportation, in addition to Isabel's fashionable Brewster carriage which had been imported, according to a newspaper account Aunt Hillary had once read aloud to Melissa and me, at tremendous expense to my father, across the Isthmus of Panama. The journalist who had reported the purchase of the carriage had not failed to note that the famous courtesan, Julia Bulette, was seen taking the air shortly thereafter in a carriage identical in every respect to Isabel's ornamental conveyance. The piece had pointed up the incongruity of life in the noisy mining community—an incongruity that threatened to overwhelm me now as I looked up warily into Marcus' handsome features that were so different from Greg's, yet alike in that they both displayed an insolent arrogance.

"My dear Julie," Marcus said gallantly. "Surely I can't seem as formidable to you as all of that."

I realized that I was staring up at him in troubled bewilderment, and flashed him a tentative smile.

Reining in his horses, he sprang down from his seat to hand me into the open carriage. "This is a pleasant surprise," he went on cordially. "I didn't expect to find you out and about at this ungodly hour. I'd have made myself available to you, if I'd known you had business to attend to so early in the morning." Curiosity darted behind his eyes, making me suddenly wary.

I said quickly, "It was nothing important."

"It's back to the nest, then?" He climbed up beside me, his gaze frankly inquisitive.

I nodded. "If that's what you like to call it." I looked skeptically at the house perched high above us at the end of the steeply winding street.

"I must admit that it isn't exactly cozy, although Isabel seemed satisfied enough with Father's efforts to please her instincts for refinement."

"Did you always call him that?" I asked when he had released the brake to send the sleek team plodding ahead, his whip licking lightly at their heaving flanks as they strained to gain a foothold on the steeply rising street. "Father?" I added, a sharply envious little pain piercing my heart.

"Does it bother you?"

"There is no reason why it should," I said.

"He was 'Father' to us, from the start, although I suspect that in the beginning it was mostly Isabel's idea. We must have seemed a motley bunch of urchins to him. I was sixteen when he married my mother, and small for my age. There were times when we were hard pressed to find enough to eat, after my real father died. I'd been the man of the family since I was eight." Marcus looked at me. "I was ready to let someone else shoulder my responsibilities. Not that the others didn't do their share willingly enough. Emma, who wasn't quite a year younger, was a help. But that's another story altogether. It has nothing at all to do with what we've since managed to make of ourselves."

And what have you managed to become, I wanted to retort, just as I had been compelled in some oddly outraged way to let Emma know that I was not unaware of her displeasure with the flirtatious looks Renny flung at me. As had happened then, I refrained from voicing the impetuous thought that shot unbidden through my mind.

Instead, I said, "It sometimes seems that Fate plays a far more important part in our lives than most of us would care to admit."

"Was it Fate that brought you to us, Julie? Or had you a hand in it yourself?" he asked.

"That depends on how you choose to look at it, I suppose," I said with dignity. "From my own point of view, it was undeniably Fate that brought me here. An unkind Fate, perhaps. But Fate, nevertheless." I thought of the letter Melissa had kept hidden from me, wondering what would have eventually become of me if I had failed to find it tucked away in the bottom of her jewelry chest. Had I been a fool to come, as I had already begun to suspect?

"Have we treated you as abominably as all of that?" Marcus was saying in a gently chiding voice.

"You've been kindly enough," I was forced to admit.

"You have to realize, if it happens that you should find us lacking in certain respects, that your sudden appearance took us all somewhat by shock."

"You were notified that I was coming," I said. "There was ample time for Isabel to wire me, had she chosen to do so. I should never have imposed myself on you if I had guessed even for a moment that I would not be welcome in my own father's house."

"You insist on sticking by your story, then."

"What else would you have me to do, under the circumstances? Lie to you about who I am? Even Gertie has seen a resemblance in me."

I had spoken hastily. Seeing the look that came onto Marcus' face, I wished belatedly that I had been more cautious. But it was too late. The harm had been done.

"So you've already succeeded in winning Gertie over to your side," he accused.

"It was her own doing."

"Did she tell you she was once in love with Father?"

"She said she had known him at a time when he was still struggling in the placers," I said.

"What else did she tell you?" A strange intensity had come over him. "What wild stories has she concocted about us, with that libelous mind of hers."

"Nothing that I had not already discovered for myself," I said.

My instinct was to save both myself and Gertie further embarrassment by avoiding any further exchange with him and I turned my attention away from his intent stare to my father's house. I could think of it no other way. In my mind's eye, it still belonged to him, even though I knew well enough that he had erected it in an effort to pacify the material cravings of the indomitable woman he had married shortly after my mother's death.

"I like to think of it as an eagle's aerie," Marcus said, following my line of vision.

"Apparently the tower room serves some such purpose," I retorted.

To my surprise, he laughed. "I'd be more apt to call it the fortress lookout," he said. "In the event we should ever have need to protect ourselves, it might come in handy."

An uneasy memory tugged at me. A sudden, sharp, cracking noise and someone shouting a desperate warning. I had turned then to see Greg Gallagher's team of prancing bays bearing down on me, his dark whip licking out at them. And later, there had been blood streaked in a dried rivulet across the shining rump of one of the sleek beasts.

"I suppose it would be easy enough to hold off the whole town from up there, if you had a store of ammunition laid by," I said cautiously, my gaze lingering on the cupola that commanded what amounted to virtually a birds-eye view of the town below, due to the abrupt rise of the mountain against which the house was shelved.

"That possibility had occurred to me," Marcus admitted in his amused way. "Isabel loathes what she refers to as our bad taste in going up there to practice our marksmanship. But in this wild country, you never know when we might have an Indian raid."

"You're not serious, of course," I remarked, cold fingers of doubt touching my neck, causing my hackles to rise as I again remembered that sharp, cracking sound which had preceded the accident that had very nearly cost me my life. Had it been a rifle, instead of a whip, I had heard that day? It would have been a simple matter for someone to take aim from the tower room to send a bullet skimming across the backs of Greg's team.

Or had it been Greg's life that had been in danger, if one of them had, indeed, climbed up to the tower room that day to practice his or her marksmanship? I did not think so. If the four of them were in the habit of climbing up to the tower room as often as Isabel's protest had seemed to imply, whoever had been there would not have been likely to miss the target on which he had set his sights that day.

"About the shooting or the Indians?" Marcus was saying, darting me an amused look.

"Neither, I should think," I said, pushing the uneasy thoughts aside.

"I don't want to intimidate you with our barbaric ways," he said. "But I'm afraid it's true that one or another of us feels compelled, from time to time, to climb up to the tower room to shoot at rabbits. The little devils are as thick as flies among the clumps of sage and headstones that dot those barren hillsides." He gestured broadly toward the barren slopes beyond the mansion.

"It sounds absolutely uncivilized," I said primly, striving to disguise the distaste I felt, mingled with an underlying sense of horror.

Which of them had it been? Marcus? Royce? Or perhaps Tim, who remained as much a mystery to me as Greg Gallagher? It was even possible, I thought bleakly, that it had been Emma, or even Isabel, in spite of the protests she had voiced against any of them using the cupola for the grim purpose Marcus had just described.

It was also possible that I was being fanciful again, searching vainly for alternatives to alleviate the suspicion that had fallen on Greg Gallagher, because of the strange fascination that I had come to feel for him.

"I'd like to teach you to shoot, if you'll let me," Marcus was saying. "Perhaps then the thought of holding a rifle in your hands and taking aim to fire won't seem quite so barbaric to you. I'm quite aware that you've been reared far more gently than any of us here."

"I know nothing at all about any of you," I heard myself saying, aware, even as I spoke, that it was the wrong thing to say and could only serve to increase whatever doubts he might have concerning me.

"Does it really matter?" Marcus said.

I turned wary eyes on him, trying to determine his meaning. It occurred to me then that if it had been Marcus who had taken aim from the tower-room windows that day, he would scarcely take it upon himself to tell me what dire purpose the queerly shaped little tower room had come to serve. Unless, of course, it was his real intention to warn me. Was it his real purpose to let me know how easily they could rid themselves of my bothersome presence, should any one of them take it upon himself to fire down on me? Had that first shot, if, indeed, it *had* been the loud crack of a rifle I had heard that day, been intended merely as a warning to send me scurrying like a frightened rabbit away from the town that had come to mean so much to my father? Furthermore, was that the real reason Emma had taken it upon herself to tell me that she had seen Loryea's ghost wandering aimlessly between the headstones of the bleakly barren cemetery? To send me running in fear for my life that seemed, suddenly, to be threatened from every side?

It would not bear thinking about, in the light of my precarious financial position, and tearing my gaze away from Marcus' pleasant smile, which I had already come to suspect served to hide his true thoughts from me, I stared out across the shining backs of the straining horses, saying in a voice that was slightly edged with bitterness,

"I suppose the tower room at the top of Greg Gallagher's house serves a similar purpose."

Marcus glanced briefly at the house that loomed above us, behind the sharply thrusting spikes that served to guard it. "That room holds its own mysteries," he said, a shadow flickering behind his smile.

"I suppose you are going to tell me next that he has his own private ghost, apart from Emma's woman in black," I retorted, more thoroughly convinced than ever that he was attempting, in his own sly way, to make me feel uneasy. Frightened.

"There would be no mystery if I knew what was hidden there," he remarked, glancing at the small room that thrust up so abruptly from the steep roof and that was as tightly shuttered as ever.

"How long have you known Greg Gallagher?" I asked, keeping my tone casual.

But I was not nearly as clever as I had hoped to be, for he darted me a brightly perceptive look, saying softly, "So you've already set your sights in that direction."

"Surely it's no crime to be curious about one's neighbors," I retorted.

"It might be a way we could have the mine back." The words, spoken in that same softly suggestive voice, stunned me.

I couldn't answer him. Fighting down a hotly rising anger, I swallowed in an effort to control my trembling throat, a small edge of my mind wondering why I should feel so outraged.

When at last I was able to speak, I said coldly, "How could that be, since you have refused to acknowledge me as a deserving member of the family?"

"It's possible that we might change our minds about you, were you to make a match with Greg Gallagher," he said, still smiling in a slightly cruel way, his eyes openly taunting me.

"You are utterly vile," I flung at him in acid tones.

Suddenly he laughed. "You're a fiery minx. And a clever one," he said, seemingly unperturbed by my sudden outburst.

"Not clever enough, perhaps," I snapped at him.

"You must be aware that you are really quite beautiful,

with that wealth of bright hair and eyes that a poet might be tempted to describe as 'emerald,'" he said. "Any man would be a fool not to want you."

"I've no intention, let alone any desire, to try to prove it one way or another," I flashed at him. "Least of all, where Greg Gallagher is concerned."

"And what of myself, Julie?" he asked boldly. "Would I stand a chance with you?"

I turned from him in distaste, his very wickedness, which was far more deviously subtle than Royce's boldly rakish advances, intriguing me against my will, making him seem suddenly treacherous. Why? I could not help wondering. Why should Marcus even dare to suggest that he might harbor romantic inclinations toward me? Or was he even more vile than I had first believed, imagining that he might use me in some devious way to gain his own treacherous ends?

Beside me, Marcus said, "You're far too beautiful to allow Greg to lock you up inside that morgue, in any case," and I found that I was staring up at Greg Gallagher's house without realizing it, caught up as I was by my own fiery emotions that filled my body with a seething tension.

I knew then that he had not taken my denials seriously, that he believed me to be like the other women he knew, or perhaps like himself, spoiled by riches and the attention that had been lavished on him as a result of them; demanding of others and convinced that he had only to express his desires for them to do his bidding. The thought filled me with frustration.

I finally said, "I have no intention of allowing myself to be locked up anywhere, for any reason whatsoever," an all too vivid memory of metal grating stealthily against metal darting through my mind.

An involuntary shudder passed over me as I recalled the terror I'd felt when I'd realized that someone who must have spied on me from one of the chilling little tower rooms and had followed me into the cemetery, slid the iron bolt into place, sealing me securely inside the vault. What did Marcus know of that night? What had caused him to refer just now to locks and morgues in connection with Greg Gallagher's house? Had he learned, through some devious means of his own, of my terrifying experience, and now hoped to frighten me further by making vague references to it that I dared not challenge? To charge in blindly in my search for answers could only serve to further endanger my life.

Yet I could not help but wonder when he said, "The entire third floor of Greg's house was sealed off two years ago." It was as if he had seen into my tumultuous thoughts and wanted to further dismay me.

Determined to keep my wits about me, I said, "I can imagine that it must get frightfully cold here during the winter months. It would be foolish for him to attempt to heat such a large house, when he lives there alone with only his housekeeper for company. Anyhow, you're wrong about the cupola being sealed off. I've seen lights there at night, burning behind those dark shutters."

Marcus gave me a shrewd look. "Are you certain about that?"

"Of course," I retorted.

"I suspect you've been listening to Emma's ghost tales," he said then, turning his attention back to the winding street that soared sharply upward beyond the walled corner of Isabel's garden, climbing steeply past the mansion to the carriage house and stables set into the hillside at the rear of the mansion.

"I know what I saw," I said, angry with him again, my rising temper causing me to reveal more of myself to him than was wise.

"Maybe Emma is right. Maybe there is a woman in black, after all," he said with an odd indifference.

I thought of the shadowy presence that had appeared in the depths of the vault, lurking beyond the pale circle of light cast by my lantern. Then vanishing as suddenly as she had appeared, fading quickly away into the very stones themselves, leaving behind her that same chilling miasma that had announced her presence and that had brushed across me like the icy fingers of death.

"According to Emma, she appears in the cemetery," I said.

"A ghost can go anywhere it pleases, or so I've been told," he said. "In which case it's not unreasonable to assume that she might feel compelled from time to time to visit the scene of the accident."

"But it happened at the mine office," I reminded him. "That is, if the ghost is Loryea's."

"I was thinking of her twin sister," Marcus said.

"Surely there aren't two of them roaming around," I said disbelievingly, wondering what he would say if I were to tell him that I had seen someone . . . something in the vault.

Would he register dismay? Disbelief? Or would he merely laugh at me.

"The two of them were inseparable, while they lived," he said.

"And Loryea's twin . . . Laura, wasn't it? . . . had been Greg Gallagher's fiancée," I said. "Which explains why, if there were such things, Loryea's ghost might want to visit his house."

Marcus glanced at me, his look, which lacked the brightly sparkling mischief I had come to associate with Royce's teasing glances, sending a warning chill through me.

I was not surprised when he said, "Loryea's sister died in that house.

"He had been heard to say on more than one occasion that Laura Labree was the only woman he would ever love," Marcus went on, when I made no response. "Perhaps it is just as well that you've no real interest in him, beyond a simple curiosity."

"How could I have, when I scarcely know the man?" I said, wanting to shout at him that I had no intention of allowing myself to fall in love with a man whose whole life was so obviously overshadowed by some darkly destructive power that reached out indiscriminately to destroy. But as appalled as I was by the catastrophic events of Greg Gallagher's life, I could not resist adding, "It must have been horrible for him, so much tragedy. . . ." my voice drifting off uncertainly when it struck me that he had, perhaps, planned it that way, after all.

"There are those who seem to invite disaster," Marcus remarked. "I suppose the real tragedy lies in the fact that others are caused to suffer for their careless deeds."

"Greg Gallagher doesn't strike me as the careless type," I said.

"Would you prefer to believe that his crimes were premeditated?"

"I know nothing about his *crimes*, as you call them. If I must believe something, I prefer to think that any deaths he may have been involved with were accidental."

"Maybe you are right," Marcus said, as if it were of no particular importance to him, one way or another. "He and Laura had argued over some minor triviality, the night she fell. She ran from him, according to the testimony Bertha Foster gave later, to go flying up the stairs to the tower. Greg pursued her, causing her to fling herself out through one of the windows in her efforts to escape from him. It was then that she lost her footing and went plummeting over the edge. Her body was perfectly impaled on one of those grotesque spikes that frame the garden. The coroner discovered later that it had pierced the poor girl's heart, killing her instantly."

I stared straight ahead, across the gleaming backs of the straining horses, overtaken by an icy horror that left me paralyzed.

Chapter FIFTEEN

The following morning I went downstairs, at Isabel's request, to find Greg Gallagher seated in the large, front parlor.

"He has had the unmitigated gall to call on you in this house," Isabel said acidly when she came to my room to fetch me. "I considered turning him away when he presented his card and asked if he might see you. But to have done so would have been uncouth, to say the least. Particularly since you are a guest beneath my room. I won't have it said that I have ever failed to treat a guest with graciousness and courtesy." Her voice was brittle with irony.

"I can't imagine what possible reason he could have for wanting to see *me*," I said nervously, feeling a flush come into my cheeks when I recalled the way he had kissed me that night in the cemetery. What could I say to such a man? How should I deport myself in the presence of one who had made such a savage claim on me?

Glancing at my reflection as I hurried past the mirrored etagere that dominated the spacious entrance hall, I nervously brushed a stray lock of hair into place, pausing briefly in an effort to control the frantic beating inside my chest before stepping through the wide, double doors, into the large room where I found him seated impatiently on a delicate, foliage-carved sofa that was dwarfed by his dominating, masculine presence.

He rose at once to greet me, reaching to take my hand briefly in his own, the low timbre of his voice wrapping itself warmly around me against my will.

"Isabel said you wished to see me," I said stiffly.

"I counted on her passion for doing the proper thing," he said. "It must have cost her something to refrain from booting me off of her doorstep, feeling as she does about me."

"Now that you are here, what is it that you want from me, Mr. Gallagher?" I asked, refusing to yield to his warm friendliness.

"I see they've wasted no time telling you about me." He smiled at me without mirth.

"What did you expect them to do? Pretend that everything that has happened, including my father's death, was entirely disassociated from you. From your house," I added tartly, recalling the hideous details of Laura Labree's death.

"If I expected anything at all, it was that you might prove to be as sensible as your father was."

"How did you know who I was that first day?" I challenged him. "You called me Julie. As if you were the one who had been expecting me."

"I recognized you the instant you stepped off of the stage," he said easily. "Your father and I were close friends, in spite of the rivalry between us. We respected each other. I had become extremely fond of him."

"Is that why you tried to run me over?" I demanded sharply.

"Surely you realize that what happened was an accident. You'd no business darting out like that so unexpectedly. I had no idea you would attempt to cross the street in that traffic."

"The freight wagons had stopped. It would have been safe enough, had it not been for you and your wild driving."

"I didn't come here to argue with you about what's over and done with," he said maddeningly.

"Why did you come, then?"

"To ask you to leave this place." His words were so entirely unexpected that I found myself gaping up at him.

"But why? Why should I, when this house belonged to my father?" I finally said.

"Because I believe your life to be in danger." His voice had dropped to scarcely more than a whisper, as if he wanted to make certain that, should any of the others be hovering nearby, none could hear him.

But it was his eyes that arrested me, as they had done that first time, shining at me out of the dim shadows. The same amber light burned behind their clear depths, possessing their own magnetic power, drawing me against my will into his sinuous intrigue.

I said, my voice dropping as his had done, "But from what quarter? Who, here, could possibly want to harm me? It's not as if I were free to simply pick up and go. Until I find the letter that I carried with me in my reticule when I arrived here, and which contained what few funds I had left to me in all the world, I can go nowhere, Mr. Gallagher. Even if I wanted to, which I don't. This is where I belong. Here, where my father chose to make his home."

"You told me of no letter," he accused.

"Because I believed you to be the one who took it," I challenged him daringly. "You are the one who found my reticule and returned it to me that day when I was struck down by your racing carriage. When I looked into my reticule, after you had returned it to me, I found that the letter was gone."

He bent toward me a little, regal in his black town coat and checked trousers that fitted tightly to show the tensile strength of his body. I was reminded, uneasily, of some fierce, jungle cat preparing to spring. It was impossible for me to read what he was thinking, to know what effect my bold challenge had had on him, apart from alerting his own zealous instincts for self-protection.

"What was in that letter?" he commanded me. "Tell me, for God's sake. I have to know."

"Surely you haven't failed to read it for yourself by now," I answered tartly.

"I can plainly see that I am getting nowhere with you," he said.

"Why should I trust you?" I demanded of him. "What do you expect me to do? Reveal myself completely to a man who is a total stranger to me?"

My stepmother's accusation against him had made a far deeper impression on me than I had so far realized, and I found myself watching him with a shrewdly calculated suspicion that must have shone in my face. When he finally spoke, his voice was grim, "You're convinced that I had something to do with your father's death, aren't you?"

"Did you?" I asked boldly.

"Not wittingly," he said.

A subtle change had come over him; a barely perceptible shadow passing behind his eyes. I had the chilling impression that he had drawn in upon himself in that same tightly shuttered way that guarded whatever secrets were hidden behind the blindly gleaming windows of the big house where he lived alone, save for the drab presence of his aging housekeeper.

Was he mad, after all? Did that explain why he had replied in such an abstruse way to my boldly blurted question? His words had seemed to imply that he was not quite certain of his own actions, that he was capable of committing deeds of violence against his own knowledge. Nor could I put from my mind the name he had called out to me inside the vault.

Loryea. For some inexplicable reason, he had mistaken me for a dead woman. Even before he had slid back the heavy bar to fling open the vault's iron doors, I had heard him calling her name, over and over again, beyond the tightly sealed panels.

"I'm afraid I don't understand," I finally said.

"There is no possible way that you could." He shook his head as if to jar loose some discomfiting memory, a pained look passing behind his grim features. "Whatever happened the night your father died is over and done with. You would do well to let it rest there."

Over and done with. Rest in peace. Rest in peace.

"Mr. Gridley said the same thing to me," I said. "It seems odd that everyone here is so determined to keep something from me. Something I feel I have every right to know."

"Some things are best left hidden," he said.

"Not when there is murder involved," I retorted.

"No one knows that for certain." He stepped toward me, reaching to take my shoulders in an iron grasp. "Let it rest!" His fingers bit into me, bruising my flesh, his black eyes flashing me some half-defined warning.

A depressive doubt lay upon me, like a thundercloud threatening to burst.

"And if I don't?" I could not resist flinging back at him even as instinct told me that to press too far with him would be to tread on dangerous ground.

"I can't be responsible for the consequences," he said.

Chapter SIXTEEN

As patiently as I could, I awaited my chance to slip through the garden to the house next door, to search for the missing letter, keeping a silent vigil behind the lace curtains that decorated my room. It seemed imperative for me to learn something of both Greg's and Mrs. Foster's domestic habits if I was to carry out, with any real hope for success, the daring task I had set for myself. I shuddered to think what might happen should Greg return home unexpectedly some evening to find me rifling through his closets and drawers. It was not a pleasing thought. Nor was I particularly pleased with my plan in general. But he had left me no other recourse, I told myself. Without the letter to prove my identity to Isabel and the Steps, I remained more or less anonymous, although I could not complain about the treatment they had given me, apart from Royce's libertine jests and Emma's sardonic comments.

Twice a week a Chinese houseboy whose room was in the laundry shed behind the mansion drove Bertha Foster down the hill to do her marketing. Furthermore, I had learned from Gertie that Bertha's room opened off a corridor behind the kitchen and that the drab little housekeeper was an extremely light sleeper, a fact which caused me some concern when I stopped to consider the gravity of my mission. I would have to rely on my own stealth to keep from waking her, I decided.

But it was Greg whom I must watch for. There seemed to be no particular pattern to his days—nor to Dr. Quinn's frequent appearances, which continued to dismay me. For I could find no conceivable reason for his visits, which were invariably carried out under the cover of darkness, as if he preferred to have them go unnoticed. I had not forgotten the peculiar undercurrent of concern that I had caught flashing between the two of them when Greg had carried me up to Dr. Quinn's office that first day, in the wake of the accident. Even then, and in spite of the fiercely throbbing pain that had jarred my head, I had sensed that they were drawn together by some underlying anxiety. It was not until after Greg had directed his attention to my inconspicuous presence that the turmoil I had seen seething nakedly behind Thomas Quinn's anxious eyes had abated, giving way to a peculiar calm.

What dreadful news had he expected Greg to bring him? Had he braced himself for tragedy when he saw Greg enter his office, because of the events in Greg's past life that seemed to mark him as a man who invited death and disaster? Then, seeing that I was still all of a piece, had he grown calm and efficient out of some swiftly rising sense of relief, in spite of the fact that he had reeked so strongly of spirits?

More than once I had glimpsed that stealthy glow glimmering faintly around the edges of the darkly varnished shutters that blinded the windows of the cupola perched astride the roof of Greg's mansion. Marcus had been wrong, I could not help thinking when that happened. The top floor of Greg's house had not been sealed off after all, following the tragic death of Loryea Labree's twin sister.

Meanwhile, the pattern of my own days had become almost routine; I watched and waited. I had fallen into the habit of sitting with Isabel and Emma in the garden during the late-afternoon hours, where the three of us gossiped pleasantly enough together while we busied ourselves with our needlework, Isabel having presented me with silken skeins of thread and a linen scarf that needed stitching to keep my hands from lying idle.

For the most part, Emma remained silent when the three of us were together in the small gazebo that had been patterned after the tower room above and that stood in the shelter of the big house, commanding a view of pastel-tinted mountains that thrust up in tiers beyond a fretwork of darkly slashing gullies and canyons. Sam had coddled several tender young vines into some semblance of lushness and they laced gently through the woven laths to form a softly sheltering bower above us. The verdant light that sifted down on us did very little to flatter Emma's colorless features, making her seem more tired and wan than ever, and I had begun to wonder if she might not have a tendency to be neurasthenic, as had Melissa. I could not help thinking then that she was more deeply concerned over Renny's gambling losses than she wanted any of us to know, which no doubt accounted for her almost constant peevishness.

On this particular day I pulled my attention away from Isabel's highly embellished account of the stylish tea she was in the habit of giving each fall to raise funds for her favorite charity, to see Emma staring vacantly at the rows of blue mountains, the ivory lace collar she was tatting lying forgotten on her lap.

When Isabel had paused for breath, I said, "On days

like this it is easy for me to see how my father grew to love this place."

"Any fondness he may have had for this place grew out of necessity." Isabel looked up from the scarf she was knitting for Royce in preparation for the winter months ahead, the soft cashmere yarn snarling around her plump fingers. "It was only because the mine is here that we decided to stay. It seemed the practical thing to do, at the time."

I could not help noticing that, for once, she had failed to remind me that whether or not I was John McKay's daughter remained still to be seen, and I could not help thinking that I was making some progress in my determination to be acknowledged as a member of my father's family.

"I'm sure he must have loved it, though," I said. "Or he should never have built this house here. Especially since he could have afforded to build anywhere he wanted to. In San Francisco, if it had struck his fancy."

"I often wish he had," Isabel said, her voice edged with bitterness.

"You imagine us to be far richer than we actually are," Emma said. "Do you think for a minute that Renny and I would stay on here if we were even half as wealthy as some people try to make us out to be? If you've come here expecting to beg a share of what we own with your false pretenses, I assure you that you are wasting your time."

"I've no intention of trying to claim anything that doesn't rightfully belong to me," I said as calmly as I could.

"Which causes me to wonder why you insist on staying on, when there is nothing here for you. Nothing at all," Emma added emphatically. "I'm certain Mother would be only too happy to provide you with stage fare to the next mining camp."

There's nothing worse than a wore-out mining camp, the fox-faced girl on the stage had said. *There's still plenty of big spenders on the lode, men like Greg Gallagher and Royce Ritchie, although they say Gallagher's a queer sort of duck. But I reckon I've handled worse. . . .*

I could not help wondering what it would be like to be as foot-loose and fancy-free as that girl had been, with nothing more pressing to worry about than how to acquire the sealskin cape she had promised herself for Christmas. But I was not that girl, nor could I ever be.

I drew a deep breath, cutting short the sudden thrust of memory. "I expect to be able to establish my identity soon," I said.

"What possible difference would it make, even if you were able to find some convincing evidence to show us," Emma retorted. "You would still be destitute."

"Perhaps not," I said recklessy, pride standing in the way of my common sense.

"I understand you paid a call on Roy Gridley," Isabel remarked casually.

I flashed her a startled look. "Who told you that?" I asked sharply.

"It wasn't Roy, if that's what you're thinking. He would never betray a client's confidence."

"Gertie," I said.

But Isabel's startled glance told me that I was wrong. Who, then? Marcus? Had he spied on me from the tower room when I had ridden off beside Gertie in Isabel's carriage? Then hurried to follow, in an effort to find out where I was going? Did that explain how he had happened onto me when I had struck off up the hill, after failing to find either Gertie or Sam along the town's crowded streets after I had left Mr. Gridley's office?

"Why should you call on Roy Gridley?" Emma demanded tartly. "You can't possibly be a client of his."

"I had some idea that anyone who chooses to do so is free to hire the services of a lawyer," I said coolly.

Emma's pale gaze bored into me. "It won't do you a bit of good," she said.

"How can you say that when you haven't the least idea why I chose to consult with Mr. Gridley in the first place," I said in that same cool voice.

"I knew when I saw you riding beside Greg Gallagher in his phaeton, that you had come here to take advantage of us," Emma said.

I was tempted to remind her that she could not possibly have known who I was, at the time, since she had not yet met me. But it did not seem worth the effort.

And so I let it rest there, the spiritless little contretemps suddenly depressing me. The pointless bouts in which Emma seemed determined to involve me could only serve to gain me nothing. I would do well, I thought listlessly, malaise settling over me like a devastating miasma, to conserve my resources until such time as I had acquired the evidence I needed to prove my case.

I was not entirely displeased when I glanced up to see Marcus approaching the small garden house along the flagstone path.

"So here you are," he said.

"You knew very well where you would find us at this hour," Emma retorted.

"A delightfully domestic little scene. Mother," he leaned to peck Isabel's powdered cheek. "And Julie, of course."

He came to sit next to me, picking up the tangle of silken thread beside me and placing it on his lap. "It's grown comfortable, having you around," he said.

I glanced sharply at him, thinking again that he was the one who had told Isabel that I had gone to see Roy Gridley. Was he being kind to me in an effort to put me off my guard? Were they all conspiring against me, with their stealthy visits to the tower room on the pretense of shooting at rabbits? While, if the truth were known, they went there to spy on my every move?

The thought made me uneasy.

I said, "I had hoped to feel comfortable in this house."

"It's impossible for any of us to feel easy here, under the circumstances," Emma said, that strange calm coming over her that I had seen in her before, making her voice sound oddly taut and strained in spite of her obvious effort to maintain control. I think I knew what she would say next, even before she spoke. "I've no idea why *she* should want to haunt this house. But I've come onto her, roaming the upstairs hall at night. It's only since you've come here, Julie, that she's decided to pay us a visit," she added, fixing her strange stare on me.

"If you imagine that I am trying in some way to intimidate you. . . ." I began, imagining, at first, that she fancied me to be the ghost.

She cut me short. "It's Loryea I've seen. There's no mistaking those black rags she wears. And the veil. . . ."

Her voice dwindled off, but not before I had caught a quiver behind it.

I thought, stunned: *She actually believes in her own wild tale.*

Beside me, Marcus laughed. "Fod God's sake, Emma. What do you hope to prove by spreading that nonsense around?"

"I know what I've seen," Emma said in that same tightly constrained way.

I only half-heard her, caught up as I was in my own chilling memory of a hazy shape shifting like a dark shadow of death through the depths of the vault.

"Your fanciful notion that you've seen her there in the cemetery near Laura's grave was bad enough," Marcus said, shaking his head. "But this. . . ." He threw up his hands in mock frustration. "Although I suppose there is no reason why she shouldn't be immortalized by a romantic legend or two. After all, she had gained some acclaim as a stage star and her flirtations were, in themselves, legendary."

"You can't deny that she was in the habit of spending long hours beside Laura's grave, while she lived," Emma said. "A habit she continues to pursue even in death. But why here? Why in this house?" She broke off, looking oddly lost and frightened.

I looked out between daintily laced tendrils and leaves at Greg's house next door. "And what of Laura?" I heard myself asking. "Does her ghost walk, too?"

Isabel, who had remained strangely silent, said, "There is as much reason for her to return to haunt him as Loryea had, if one wants to believe such things are possible."

Him. She meant Greg Gallagher, of course. I had only to look at her face, which had tightened into acid lines around her small mouth, to guess as much.

Her voice, when she spoke again, was edged with disfavor. "Personally, I have no taste for this sort of idle gossip." Gathering up her needles and yarn, she rose to go, her back stiff as she hurried off along the flagstone walk.

"You've upset Mother with your wild talk," Marcus scolded Emma, when she had gone.

"You're a fool if you don't believe me," Emma retorted peevishly.

"What can a ghost do?" Marcus shrugged.

"It's not inconceivable to imagine that they've both risen from their graves to walk," Emma said, her blank expression suggesting that she had become lost again in her own dark thoughts. "After Laura died there were rumors that Greg had flown into a rage and pushed her. But why should either of them come here to this house? Why?"

I continued to look out at the house next door, my gaze going to the darkly shuttered cupola. What had happened there, the night Laura Labree had slipped on the roof to go flying onto the cruel spikes below? Did Greg climb up to the little room in some futile attempt to expiate himself for having been responsible for her tragic death? Did that explain the faint rim of light I had seen seeping past the closed shutters that gave the stylish mansion a darkly blinded look, as if it had turned in upon itself in a fit of morbid brooding? And what of Thomas Quinn? It was only on those nights when he had appeared, riding crookedly up the steep street on the back of his tired horse, that I had seen the light. Was Greg's guilt so great that he could not cope with it alone? And knowing that, did Dr. Quinn ride up the hill to administer him some potent narcotic that gave him a temporary peace from his own morbid brooding?

"It would never do for you to become bemused by a man like Greg Gallagher," Marcus said.

I looked away from the brooding house to find him watching me.

"You make him out to be a bluebeard," I said.

"Julie, darling. I'm only trying to save you from yourself. If you must pursue thoughts of Greg Gallagher, let them be for practical reasons. That way, you won't be hurt or disappointed when he proves to be something less than you had imagined."

"If I had been inclined to pursue thoughts of any man, I should have done so long before this," I said, suddenly angry with myself for having been so transparent as to have allowed Marcus to see into my emotions, which had become so hopelessly tangled that not even I could sort them out to any degree of satisfaction.

"You present a challenge," Marcus said wickedly, as Royce might have done.

I laid aside my embroidery when he had gone, leaving me alone with Emma, who continued to brood in silence, moving her shuttle absently in and out through the loops of ivory-colored thread that she had wound loosely around her fingers.

Staring out wistfully at the distant mountains, I was overwhelmed by the sudden thought that my father must have gazed out often on the rugged scene, just as I was doing now, his eye tracking the ragged pattern of the diggings that scarred their smooth flanks, the raw-waste dumps spilling in pale streaks above the deep gullies.

Although the McKay-Ritchie was not visible to me from that angle, I had seen the main shaft house from the mansion's second-story windows, thrusting up boldly above the steep face of the mountain.

I had noticed at the same time a faint track winding away from the mansion, beyond the carriage house and stable, twisting up the hillside between silvery clumps of sage and rabbit brush in the direction of the mine. Was that the route my father had taken that night? I wondered now. Had he climbed through darkness to the isolated shaft house, only to die there alone, pinned hopelessly to the floor of the cage that was used to lower the miners into the deep drifts?

An aching lump formed in my throat and, hastily excusing myself to Emma, I hurried off along the flagstone walk, aware that she had raised her pale eyes to stare curiously after me.

Running up the front stairs to my room, I tied on my bonnet, and going to the narrow window at the end of the short corridor that bisected the main hallway which passed by my room, I traced with my eye the rugged little trail that led up to the mine, following it as far as I could see, between rough patches of brush. A short distance beyond the roof of the carriage house, which crouched below the narrow dips and turns, the path disappeared into a deep gully, emerging again on its far side to shoot upward between the scraggly bushes that carpeted the mountain's steep flanks like a moth-eaten hide.

I knew where I was going, and turning determinedly about, I ran down the stairs, oblivious to Gertie's curious look as I shot past the kitchen and out into the back yard, all but colliding with Sam, who scuttled by me on silent feet, his slight form dwarfed by the dripping buckets of water that dangled from his wooden yoke.

Chapter SEVENTEEN

An occasional stunted pine tree had survived the miners' onslaught to cast its sketchy shadow across the narrow little track that wound along the hillside, above the two mansions. Picking up my skirts, I followed the twisting little trail down the rocky wall of a deep, narrow gully, small puffs of red dust rising from beneath my flying feet.

When I had climbed as quickly as I could up the far side of the small canyon, lifting skirts that were already laden with tiny, clinging seeds above the tips of my dusty shoes, I dared to glance nervously back across my shoulder at the twin cupolas that thrust above the town, the cloudless sky reflected in their darkly shimmering windows. As had happened before, I had the sensation that someone watched from behind their flickering panes, but I could no longer be certain which of the two houses concealed that half-sensed evil that sent a queer little shiver down my spine.

Bending low behind the dusty clumps of sage, I hurried on, past wooden trestles that held sagging chutes, along which waste ore had once rumbled to go flying out through their open ends onto the monstrous dumps that spilled down the steep slopes, threatening to engulf the town. The trail passed beneath the weathered flumes, scattered here with stones that had spilled out through breaks in the weathered boards so that I was forced to pick my way carefully past small heaps of rubble.

Climbing beyond the trestled troughs, I paused to catch my breath, my gaze going to the shaft house that loomed beyond yet another of the deeply slashing gullies that scarred the face of the mountain. The mine was farther away than I had anticipated. But now that I had made up my mind to go there, I would not turn back, and flashing yet another look at the houses below me, I had started to go on when the back door to my father's mansion was flung open and Royce emerged, followed closely by Renny and Isabel. The three of them appeared to be arguing, Royce's hands flying up in a familiar gesture of acquiescence before he hurried on toward the carriage house, Renny following in his shadow. Isabel stayed where she was for a moment or two longer, suddenly seeming to stare straight at me, and for a stunned instant I imagined that her piercing gaze had found me.

Huddling behind a pungent clump of rabbit brush, the yellow blooms brushing my cheeks, I continued to peer through the sparse foliage at the house below, seeing Isabel turn, at last, to disappear into the mansion. Neither Royce nor Renny were visible to me now, having gone into the carriage house, and seizing my opportunity to escape unnoticed from my hiding place, I darted down the sharp incline, reaching to steady myself against a stony outcropping.

The trail zigzagged downward into the gully, which was larger than the first, its rocky walls laced with animal runs that branched away from the main path at unevenly spaced intervals to penetrate the rugged scrub.

The bottom of the gully was strewn with waist-high boulders, attesting to the fierceness of the flash floods that surged through the small canyons during the spring months when the winter snows had begun to thaw, and I thought that I would not like to be caught scrambling across the face of the mountain then, as I passed by the broken remains of a small trestle bridge that had given way beneath that powerful onslaught.

Even now, during the dry months of summer, the going was precarious even at best. I had started to climb again, zigzagging slowly up the far side of the gully, when a ction of the narrow trail spilled away from beneath my et and I went flying, clutching at the wiry tufts of brush break my fall. Rivulets of stone plummeted down on e, a rock the size of my fist thudding, with a force that used me to utter an involuntary little cry, against my nkle. It was the same ankle that I had twisted that night hen I'd gone to the vault and I lay nursing the bruised one, tears of pain and frustration dimming my eyes. Vhen at last that fiercely probing ache had subsided, I athered myself up, attempting to brush the prickly little eeds from my gown, which was the same one I'd worn hen I had visited my father's tomb and was already a it the worse for wear, in spite of my efforts to revive , using Gertie's sadirons and a steam cloth. The matches had put into my pocket that night were still intact, aving been replaced by me when I had finished pressing ne dress. I wanted to be ready, should my chance to ip through the garden to search Greg's mansion arise nexpectedly.

Now, gingerly testing my bruised ankle, I struck off up ne trail at a cautious pace, alerted for loose stones that ould send me sprawling. I had gone perhaps a dozen ards, winding back and forth at a snail's pace up the vall of the small canyon, when it suddenly occurred to ne that I was no longer alone on the mountain. I have o idea how long I had lain in the rough grass below the rail, nursing my hurting ankle. Nor even how I knew that was being followed. There was nothing, beyond my own nstincts, to warn me, no sudden sound shattering the tillness around me; no sharp rattle of falling stones to nark another person's stealthy ascent along the steep idges.

Yet I knew, in that same way that a wild creature seems o sense that it is being stalked by the hunter, that there vas another presence nearby and that whoever . . . whatever it was that lurked there was evil.

Had one of them seen me leave the mansion, after all, nd decided to follow me? If so, who? Which of them vas it? If he or she had wanted to harm me, it would nave been a simple matter to take careful aim from the ower windows, to send a bullet speeding through my neart. I did not doubt for an instant that I had presented a tempting target to any who were accustomed to shooting rabbits at random from behind those darkly glittering panes, as I scurried along the thickly grown path. Why bother to follow me, then? Why not have had it over and done with quickly, if whoever it was wanted to kill me?

Or was it another kind of danger that I faced? Had Royce glimpsed me from the yard below and decided to come after me? It was a discomfiting thought, for I did not doubt for an instant that he was a man who would attempt to take full advantage of the situation, should he come onto me alone.

But when I had clawed my way around the final turn in the trail that took me out of the gully onto the mountain's main slope, I saw no one. I stayed where I was, my gaze going the length of the trestle and the gully beyond. Did someone lurk behind the giant slag heaps? I listened, aware that it would be virtually impossible for anyone to attempt to pass along their sprawling bases without stirring loose a stone. But there was no sound to break the late afternoon stillness, only the far-off shrieking of a bird rising above the soft, rustling drone of the insects that worked among the pungent blooms.

Starting on again, I cast a wary look across my shoulder from time to time, a vague sense of uneasiness still possessing me.

I was within a few feet of the shaft house when there was a sudden, sharp rattle of stones behind me and I whirled swiftly about in time to see a small puff of red dust rise slowly out of the gully through which I had just passed. I froze in my tracks, waiting for whoever was there to show himself, aware that by stooping low, a man could easily conceal himself behind the stiff rows of brush that guarded the narrow trail. The thought of one of them slinking after me like a crouching coyote caused the hackles on my neck to rise, and whirling swiftly about, I ran as fast as I could toward the looming shaft house.

I did not stop until I was leaning breathlessly against the gray planks that enclosed the tall headframe. Only then did I dare to look back the way I had come, to see a tawny antelope come bounding up out of the gully. The agile creature went jumping off through the thick clumps of sage, small clouds of red dust rising at its heels. I watched the graceful animal vanish, wondering what had startled the shy creature. That same lurking evil that I had sensed?

Even as I watched, a second, tawny shape came bounding up out of the gully to go leaping after the racing antelope. My heart jumped into my throat when I saw that it was some kind of mountain cat, intent on bringing down its prey.

The presence of the two beasts seemed to explain my own feeling of uneasiness and I whirled away from that primitive scene, sliding swiftly between plank doors that hung askew on overhead rollers, into the dim recesses of the hugely looming shaft house.

I turned slowly about, waiting for my eyes to adjust to the thick gloom. An ell opened off at one side of the main room, a greasy engine crouching in its black shadows like some grotesque beast that had crawled into its cave to hibernate. Wire hoisting ropes laced between the engine and a large wheel mounted high above me, at the top of the towering headframe, and passed over it to drop between the monstrous beams that supported the whole, strange mechanism.

It was then that I saw the cage, suspended from the heavy, braided wire, scarcely more than a simple platform enclosed with wire mesh, hanging precariously over a bottomless pit that fell away abruptly at my feet, and a strange sickness took hold of me, turning my knees to water. Several pieces of rod lay on the wooden platform that surrounded the dark hole, and I knew, without being told, that they were lengths of drill steel, similar to the one that had plummeted into the shaft to pierce my father's body, pinning him helplessly to the cage's plank floor.

It was as if whoever had last visited the isolated shaft house had purposely arranged the torturous instruments for my inspection, so that I was suddenly able to visualize my father's senseless death with a jarring clarity. Governed by that same sick sense of horror, I went on watery knees to peer into the cage, as if by doing so I could find an answer to the darkly seething doubts that haunted me.

Wooden, rail-like guides ran down the shaft, disappearing into darkness to hold the cage in alignment, and there was a safety brake attached to one side, its wooden handle worn smooth with use. If there were dark stains on the plank floor of the small elevator, they were mercifully lost to me in that poor light.

I had started to draw away when I heard it: a footstep falling softly behind me. I spun around to see a dark shadow plummeting toward me like some giant bird, its wings spread wide to sweep me head first into the rickety cage. The cage bounced precariously on its wire rope as I went sliding across splintery boards, my head coming to rest with a hollow thud against one of the worn guide posts. The sudden jolt sent a shaft of pain glancing through my temple, a wave of dizziness, overwhelming me, shot through with a myriad dancing stars that blinded me.

I stayed where I was, unable to help myself even as a small, horror-numbed corner of my mind waited with a dreadful patience for the swiftly darting length of steel that I was certain would come flying in at me, to pin me like a helpless butterfly to the rough floor of the cage.

I was only vaguely aware of that darkly flitting shadow that hovered briefly above me, hissing at me in a hoarsely inhuman voice, "I tried to warn you. But you wouldn't listen, would you? You wouldn't take heed. I have no choice now but to kill you. This time, I promise you I won't fail."

A queer, scraping sound, followed by a loud, clanking noise, penetrated my numbed senses. The cage door closing on rusted hinges, followed by the sound of a bolt being slammed violently into place. . . .

I opened my eyes, staring out dizzily through the close-knit mesh at a darkly wavering shape that moved swiftly away from me. Blinking my eyes in an attempt to focus my vision, I watched that chilling form fade slowly into the deep shadows beyond the giant engine that dominated the ell, thinking vaguely that she had found me again. For there was no mistaking her, clad as she was in the black garb of mourning, a heavy veil falling to her waist to hide her formless features from me.

I must have fainted briefly, for the next thing I knew, a sudden, sharp snapping sound jarred through my numbed senses and I sat up with a start, the gentle tones of a man's voice echoing softly through my head: *silly little minx, dashing out like that.*

For a stunned instant, I imagined myself to be back in the dusty street, the familiar creak of straining leather, accompanied by the restless stamp of horses' hooves, echoing around me. My arm flew up to ward off danger.

But I was too late. For suddenly I was plunging downward, into darkness, the cage jolting beneath me, flinging me headlong against the wire screen. Vaguely, it occurred to me that the sudden, sharp noise I had heard had been the snap of a wire rope.

Panic-stricken, I clawed at the wire meshes, trying to right myself. But it was no use. The terrible force of the falling cage had rendered me helpless and I lay pinned against the rough boards, thinking numbly that this time, the woman in black had won, even as I waited for the final jarring jolt to snuff out my life.

I have no idea what caused the cage to suddenly slow its pace, the wooden frame grinding loudly against the thick, guiding beams. A spill of ore, perhaps, that had fallen into the shaft to clog the rails. Whatever the reason, I became slowly aware that it had slackened its breakneck speed, and I was able then to get to my feet, a spark of hope burgeoning to send me lunging blindly through darkness to fling my full weight against the worn handle of the safety brake.

There was a splintering crash as the worn mechanism jammed into place, slowing the pace of the falling cage that landed, in the next instant, with a sudden, jarring smash that threw me off of my feet.

Somewhere nearby, water dripped, the small, splashing sounds rippling softly around me. Slowly, I uncoiled my arms from around my head and extended aching legs, my body unfolding like that of a newly hatched chick breaking free from its shell. Except that there was no bright new world to greet me. Only a smothering darkness that wrapped itself around my bruised body like a cold, moist blanket.

Nevertheless, it occurred to me then that I was still alive.

Chapter EIGHTEEN

I fumbled in the pocket of my gown for the matches I had put there when I'd attempted to restore the dress to some semblance of respectability, following my adventure in the vault. Striking one of the sulphurous little sticks, I saw that the cage door had flown open, upon impact, and I stepped out into a rock-lined tunnel, the flickering flame nipping at my fingers. Tossing the match onto the plank ramp that led to the door of the cage, I watched it flicker out, plunging me into a darkness so thick that I had the eerie sensation of a solid wall forming around me.

Reaching for yet another match from my precious store, I struck it against the stone wall, my gaze searching frantically for a lantern or candle left behind by the miners when the shaft had been abandoned.

But there were only the gray rock walls leading away on either side of me, beyond the heavy beams that supported the wire-screened cage. Touching the tiny flame to one of the thick posts, I blew gently on the licking tongue of fire in an attempt to ignite the splintery wood, ignoring Mr. Gridley's dramatic account of the fires that surged out of control in the depths of the mines, endangering countless lives. If there had been a fire in the mine the night my father died, it had been on one of the lower levels, where the subterranean gases posed a constant hazard. Secure in that thought, I nursed the tiny spark of fire, only to have it die just as I fancied that it had caught, plunging me again into darkness.

Somewhere high above me, someone laughed. Feeling my way back into the cage, I stared upward, making out a faint square of light high above me.

Did I dare to hope that I could deal with madness? Staring upward, past the beams that criss-crossed at the top of the cage and to which the wire rope had been attached, I called out loudly, knowing that whatever the consequences might prove to be, I had, at least, to try.

"Loryea?" The sound of my voice faded almost immediately, absorbed by the earthen walls. I called again, "Loryea?"

Someone leaned above me over the shaft's opening, blotting out the faint square of light.

"I fooled you, didn't I?" that same hoarsely disguised voice called down to me. "You thought I was Loryea. But I'm not, do you understand? Loryea is dead. Dead! Just as you, too, must die. No one will ever think to look for you down there. It's only a matter of time before you'll be dead, like Loryea."

"I'll be missed," I called up to that shadowy form that continued to hover over the mouth of the mine. "A party will be organized to search for me. The mine is the first place they'll think to look."

"Do you think they give a damn what happens to you?" my accoster shot back at me in scathing tones. "There isn't one of them who won't be glad to be rid of your bothersome presence here."

"You're wrong about that," I shouted desperately. The hollow sound of my own voice seemed suddenly to mock me. Nevertheless, I said, "There are those who care about what happens to me."

"Who? Who could possibly care?" that other voice said.

"Royce, for one. Marcus. Even Renny," I shot back at the person who crouched high above me, at the edge of the pit.

"No one cares, do you understand?" whoever it was spat angrily down at me. "No one!"

I saw then that it was no use and I fell silent, thinking grimly that if I was to escape from the trap I had fallen into, I must find my own way out through the maze of drifts and tunnels that formed a pattern, like a giant spider's web, beneath the mountain.

Peering upward, I saw that whoever had been there had gone, and a chilling sense of desolation took hold of me. Then, without warning, that tiny, unattainable square of light was blotted out by some dark object that came plummeting down at me. Instinctively flinging my arms around my head in a protective gesture, I stepped backward, my heel catching on the edge of the cage, sending me sprawling directly in the path of that wildly flying dark blur that settled over me like a smothering cloud.

I knew then what it was and I pushed aside the soft folds of dark cloth, thinking crazily: The woman in black is dead.

I remembered what Mr. Gridley had told me concerning the terrible fires that raged out of control in the mines and, slowly, a daring plan began to form in the back of my mind. Laying aside the voluminous veil my accoster had worn, I twisted the soft cloth of the dress into a torch. Feeling in my pocket for a match, I struck the white-tipped head against one of the splintery planks, holding the tiny flame to the black cotton cloth, blowing softly on it to stir it into a blaze. Then, laying the makeshift torch beneath the edge of a board that was streaked faintly with pitch, I stood aside, waiting nervously for it to catch.

The fire flared, eating away at the tightly woven fabric, the dancing flames illuminating the tunnel behind me. The water I had heard earlier formed a glistening rivulet that flowed across the rough floor to form sparkling little pools beneath my feet. Metal ore cars stood nearby, where they had been abandoned on lengths of steel track, and there was a small room opening off of the main corridor a short distance beyond where I stood. One of the infirmaries Mr. Gridley had told me about, I decided, making my way swiftly toward the arched opening.

Reaching into my pocket for the last of my matches, I struck the flimsy little stick against the gray rock and peered inside, my gaze going at once to the candle that stood nearby on a small table. Touching the small blaze to the candle's singed string, I nursed it into a steadily burning tongue of flame, turning then to see a shelf that held an assortment of tins and bottles and a low cot standing against the back of the room, a gray, flannel blanket neatly folded at its foot. There was no time to see what the tins held. But it was comforting to know that the cot with its folded blanket was there in the event that my rescuers failed to appear as quickly as I anticipated, for already a damp chill had begun to seep through me, turning my fingers numb.

The fire I had started, using the black dress that my accoster had hurled down at me, had begun to burn in earnest when I stepped again into the main tunnel, the dancing flames licking hungrily at the pitchy board, the streamers of black smoke beginning to curl upward into the main shaft.

Who would be the first to see those telltale black tendrils winding above the shaft house? I wondered. My accoster? I shivered at that frightening possibility, telling myself that he would not be the only one to notice a dark smudge darkening the sky above the mountain. Surely others would be watching. I already knew what I would tell my rescuers. I was not yet ready to go flinging accusations wildly about.

The flames leaped higher, threatening to envelope the cage as the draft that surged through the tunnel whipped them upward and I knelt to soak the black veil in one of the small pools, then wrung the cold water onto the dancing flames, bringing them quickly under control. Again and again I went with the soaked veil, squeezing water onto the fire, deftly controlling the small blaze until I was certain that it had served its purpose.

But I was not nearly so clever as I had wanted to believe. For when help finally came, it was Greg Gallagher's voice that called down to me.

"Who's there?" he demanded to know, the angry sound of his voice bouncing off of the stone walls of the shaft to echo accusingly around me. "Who in hell has tampered with this cage?"

I had no choice but to answer him.

I watched him descend, finding hand and foot holds in the huge beams that served as guides for the cage, his daring filling me with a peculiar dread.

But he was far more sure of himself than I was.

He brushed rudely by me, when he had alighted, going quickly to fetch a bucket from one of the ore cars and, filling it swiftly from one of the small pools, returning to drown the flickering tongues of flame that licked fruitlessly at the thick cage guides.

"That was a damn fool thing to do," he said then,

crunching the last of the smoldering coals beneath his boot. "My god, do you realize what could have happened, had that fire gone out of control? I dread to think of the conflagration you might have caused, had the draft switched suddenly to draw those flames into the lower levels." He shook his head in disgust, the candle that burned in a holder attached to the front of his canvas cap flaring violently.

Moving with that same deft sureness that had brought him safely down the shaft, he climbed to the top of the cage, his fingers flying to mend the broken rope, securing it stoutly to the cross beams.

Ordering me gruffly aside, he began to climb, disappearing into the dim shadows above my head. A moment or two later, I heard the engine I had seen crouching in the ell sputter to life, and after another brief hesitation, during which I caught the sound of hissing steam, the cage began to climb slowly.

I was still clinging tightly to the water-soaked veil when he brought me to the surface. Stepping gingerly from the cage onto the wooden platform, I was stunned to discover that darkness had begun to fall. It occurred to me then that I was alone on the mountain with a man who might very well be mad, and a queer sensation of dread went through me, coupled with a peculiar feeling of excitement.

I could not deny the attraction he held for me, when he appeared in the doorway of the ell, his lean, brown face oddly illuminated by the flickering candle.

"What am I to do with you?" he said then. "You seem bent on destroying yourself and there appears to be very little I can do to stop you."

"I assure you that it was not my intention to go plunging into that terrible shaft when I came up here," I said heatedly. "If you had kept the cage in repair, such a frightful thing could never have happened," I went on recklessly, aware, even as I spoke, that I was being unfair.

At the same time, it did not seem inconceivable, under the circumstances, to believe that it might have been Greg who had masqueraded as the woman in black, slipping up the side of the mountain behind me to push me into the flimsy cage when I stooped to examine it, as he surely must have known I would do, considering that my father had died there.

Then, while I'd lain stunned on the plank floor inside the wire-mesh screen, going into the engine room to sever the wire rope and send me plunging helplessly into the black pit that yawned below the platform on which I now stood. I shuddered at that terrifying memory, wondering, in the next breath, why he had bothered to come back at all if it had been his real intention to get rid of me. Was it because I had set fire to his precious mine? Was there nothing quite so important to him as the McKay-Ritchie, just as Isabel and the Steps had led me to believe, so that he had felt compelled to return when he saw smoke trailing above the shaft house, to save it from a conflagration that could smolder through the lower levels for years should the fire happen to spread? Apparently no one else had glimpsed the dark threads of smoke rising above the mine, due to the rapidly descending darkness, which only served to add to my suspicions.

He came slowly toward me and I posed myself for flight, the veil trailing damply beside me.

"What is that soggy mess you're hanging on to so desperately?" he asked suspiciously, reaching to snatch the limp folds from my fingers. Spreading the veil before him, so that the candlelight fell across its shimmering wetness, he stared into my face. "Where did you get this?" he demanded harshly.

"Do you know whose it is?" I asked as calmly as I could.

He carefully folded the wet veil and tucked it into his shirt pocket. "I've seen it before," he said guardedly.

"It was hers, wasn't it?" I could not stop myself from saying. "Loryea Labree's."

He turned to go, pretending that he had not heard me.

"Well?" I said, following him out into the last faint glow of a deepening dusk.

He turned so quickly that I could not stop myself from bumping against him. Before I could pull away, his arms reached to encircle me.

"Go away from here, Julie," he whispered. "Go away, at least for a little while. Give me time. . . ." His voice faded, the soft rise and fall of his breath gently stirring my hair.

Go away. Go away, the shadowy form that I had encountered in the depths of the vault had commanded me.

"Why?" I whispered, when at last he had released me, giving a savage little shake of his head as if to clear away some darkly haunting memory. "Why must I leave here?"

"I have no real right to ask this of you," he said. "Yet, I must, for your own protection. Perhaps someday you will come to understand."

"Understand what?" I persisted in that same frightened whisper. "I have to know what danger lurks here, since I have nowhere else to go. Is it you I must fear? Tell me. I can't possibly understand where the danger lies unless I know what it is I must fear."

"I can't do that," he said grimly. "Not yet. Not for a while."

"But if I leave here, we shall never see each other again." An underlying emotion that I did not dare yet to define caused my voice to tremble.

"Let me take you away from here," he said in a voice that was edged with a queer desperation. "To San Francisco. I have a small house there where I stay when I visit the city on business. I'll find a respectable woman to look after you. You can stay there until . . . until the new gown I promised you is ready." His voice became inspired, its soft tone boldly luring me. "You see, I haven't forgotten that I owe you a new travel costume and it happens that the best dressmaker I know of is located there."

I stared up numbly at his face, which was scarcely more than a shadow in that swiftly failing light. "You must be mad," I whispered. "Mad!"

"Why? Because it is my wish to repay a debt I owe?"

"You owe me nothing, do you understand? Nothing at all!" With that, I flung myself away from him, flying recklessly down the hillside as if death itself were chasing me.

Chapter NINETEEN

There was nothing in any of their faces to give them away when, after making myself as presentable as possible, I went downstairs to confront them. I thought then that if it had been one of them who had followed me to the mine, that person was decidedly clever.

I had found them in the front parlor, where apparently they had gathered to hear Emma play. It had been the sound of the piano that had told me where they were, when I had flung myself through the mansion's back door, casting a last frantic look across my shoulder to make certain that Greg Gallagher had not taken it upon himself to follow me.

It was Marcus who said, "You're late for dinner, Julie. I'm afraid the rest of us have already finished."

"I'm not hungry," I said.

"Nonsense." Isabel reached for the fringed bellpull beside her chair.

None of them had bothered to ask me where I had been nor had questioned my absence in any way, and it crossed my mind then, as it had before, that they were all conspiring against me. Suddenly, I could not escape from them quickly enough and I turned to go, all but crashing into Sam, who had appeared on silent feet, standing in bowed subservience to await Isabel's bidding.

"Julie?" my stepmother called after me when I turned to fling myself back up the stairs.

I pretended not to hear her.

I had the chilling sensation, as I bounded up the stairs, my bedraggled skirts clutched above my shoetops, that the evil I had sensed lurking behind the glaring windows of the two houses that seemed to rival each other for predominance over the thriving mining community was closing rapidly around me. A strange restlessness had taken hold of me and, alone again in my room, I found myself restlessly pacing the floor in an effort to determine which way I should turn.

I was still roaming nervously between the big bed and the lace-covered windows that continued to draw me because of that other house that stood below my father's, when there was a soft rap on the door. I opened it to find Isabel standing outside in the hallway, a linen-covered tray in her plump hands.

"Something happened this evening," she said abruptly, pushing past me to deposit the tray on the marble-topped table that stood near the carved setee.

"How did you know?" I searched her face for some betraying flicker of guilt, wondering if it were possible, after all, that she was the one who had followed me.

"It's plain to see you're agitated," she said. She hesitated, then went on in a low, tense voice. "Is it Royce? Or perhaps Renny? Has one of them tried to . . . molest you?"

For a piercing moment, I stood staring at her.

Then, finally, I said, "Why should you think such a thing? Surely you can't imagine that I would permit either of them to . . . to take advantage of me."

"I know my son and Emma's husband," she stated flatly.

"And I know myself," I said with spirit. "Whatever gave you such an idea?"

"I have my ways to know what takes place in this house," she said, stooping to arrange the tray's contents, carefully arranging the heavy silver and laying a warming cover aside to reveal moist, red slices of roast beef. "It won't do for you to go wandering off alone after this. If you wish to continue on here as my guest, you must agree to conduct yourself with some sense of propriety. I won't have you courting idle gossip with your reckless behavior."

I said, reining in my temper, "I haven't the least desire to bring shame on myself. Or my father's memory," I added impulsively.

"I'm glad to hear that you intend to make some effort to be discreet in the future." Her tone was slightly mocking, her dark stare piercing into me. "What if someone else had seen you?"

"I've no idea what you're talking about," I said.

"I know that you followed the trail that leads up to the shaft house, after you left the gazebo," she said accusingly. "I also know that someone joined you there later."

I gave her an appalled stare. "You were spying on me from the tower room," I challenged her. "You or one of the others. Which of you was it? Who stood by and did nothing while I faced death up there alone?"

"Don't be dramatic," she snapped. "You must have known what you were getting yourself into when you agreed to meet him there. Surely, you can't expect a man to show respect for you after you have committed yourself to meet him clandestinely. It's quite obvious to me that you are no longer a child."

"But I had agreed to meet no one," I said with asperity. "I went there out of curiosity, to see the mine. If you imagine that I went there to meet someone, you have been badly misinformed."

I saw that my words had reached her, for she hesitated. When she finally spoke, she sounded less sure of herself, and I knew then that it had been one of the others who had seen me on the trail and had gone tattling to Isabel, for his or her own devious reasons.

"Please, we'll say no more about your little escapade," she said. "But I am warning you, Julie. Should anything like it ever happen again, I shall be forced to ask you to leave this house."

With that she left me, and I sat staring blindly at the door she had shut firmly behind her, wondering again which of them it had been. Who had gone running to Isabel to tell her that I had been seen striking off up the mountain along the winding little trail that led to the shaft house? Royce? Renny? Both of them had been in a position to see me, half-hidden as I had been by the sparse clumps of rabbit brush.

Marcus had had equal opportunity to catch a glimpse of me, if it happened that he had suddenly decided to climb the stairs that led up to the tower room, to shoot at rabbits. I shuddered to think that he might have been there behind the dark panes, peering at me along the barrel of his rifle.

And what of Tim? It was not wholly implausible to believe that he might have come riding in from his claim earlier than usual, to see me flitting swiftly along the steep little path that circumvented the mountain above the two houses.

Even Emma was not above suspicion. Had she climbed to the tower room to spy on Renny, as Royce had claimed was her habit, and had she then seen one of them following me? Did that explain why Isabel had felt compelled to ask if one of them had attempted to molest me, as she had so delicately put it?

Nor could I completely disregard the possibility that it might have been Isabel, after all, who had observed my movements from the mansion's second-story windows. It had taken me at least a half-hour, perhaps longer, to reach the shaft house. There had been ample time for her to slip up the stairs, after I saw her leave Royce and Renny, to peer out from behind the thin curtains in an effort to determine where I was off to. It was not the sort of thing Isabel would willingly admit to. Yet I did not doubt for an instant that she was not above spying on others, should it occur to her that to do so might somehow serve her own cause—and if she could be equally certain that she would not be found out. There is a bit of chicanery in all of us and I did not imagine Isabel to be exempt, for all of her carefully cultivated airs.

I was all too acutely aware that both Isabel and the Steps suspected me of having devious plans of my own. Nor was Greg Gallagher entirely indifferent to what I did. He had as much as admitted to me that he found my presence discomfiting. If it had been Greg who had taken the missing letter from my reticule, as I had led myself to believe, he was every bit as aware as I was that my father had intended to leave me a legacy. It remained only for me to find the document that my father had prepared on the night of his death for me to state my claim. Did that claim somehow affect the ownership of the McKay-Ritchie Mine that now belonged to Greg Gallagher? Did that explain why he seemed so determined to have me out of the way, if only for a short while, as the shocking proposition he had made to me in the shaft house had seemed to suggest?

Under the circumstances, it behooved them all to keep a close watch on me, I could not help thinking, a queer little shiver passing over me. Someone had watched. And had followed, of that much I was certain. But who? Which of them stood to gain the most, if I should one day be found dead, as my father had been.

As had become my habit, I went to the bay windows to stare out through the ornate lace at the house below. Lights burned dimly behind the second-floor windows, warning me that Greg was at home. My decision to slip through Isabel's garden, under cover of darkness, to search for the missing letter would have to be postponed for yet another night. A peculiar ambivalence took hold of me, for I did not relish the dangerous task I had set for myself. Yet I knew that it was something I must do, if I was to have the proof I needed to establish my identity as John McKay's daughter.

Blowing out my candle, I disrobed for bed, slipping gratefully into my soft, cambric nightdress. My body ached from my ordeal in the mine shaft and I crawled eagerly between crisp, linen sheets that smelled pleasantly of lavender from Isabel's garden.

But sleep eluded me, beset as I was by my own dark doubts.

I have no idea how long I lay in the big bed, tossing and turning from side to side in an effort to make my bruised body more comfortable, attempting to put the teeming barrage of haunting questions from my mind.

When at last I admitted to myself that I was getting nowhere, that I was only agitating myself further by consciously waiting for sleep to come to me, I decided that what I needed most to relax me was a glass of warm milk from Gertie's spotless kitchen. Slipping from the big bed, I slid my arms into the lush sleeves of the velvet robe Melissa had given me at the last minute, fastening the soft, mink collar snugly against my throat, taking a peculiar comfort from the fur's silken opulence.

Going to the door in darkness, I twisted the silver knob and stepped as quietly as I could out into the hallway, softly drawing the heavy panels closed behind me. I had no desire to wake the others, particularly Royce, who had apparently decided, for reasons of his own, to forgo his usual nightly pleasures. I had heard him pass by my door earlier, on the way to his room, which was located some distance from my own, past a turn in the long corridor, as was the room that Emma and Renny shared, on those nights when the flirtatious Italian deigned to remain at home in lieu of going off with Royce at the first hint of nightfall to indulge his own Sybaritic tastes.

Marcus, Tim, and Isabel had rooms in the opposite wing, so that I was alone in the main section of the big house that seemed suddenly to be filled with a myriad haunting shadows.

One of the shadows moved as I started down the stairs, stepping forward to block my progress. Stifling a scream, I saw in the faint light from the lamp that Gertie had left burning in a bracket on the landing that it was Renny. His reeking breath told me that he had sampled far too generously the store of spirits that Royce kept in the dining room sideboard to serve to his infrequent guests. Murmuring a breathless apology, when I inadvertently bumped against him on the narrow flight, I attempted to pass by him.

But he was not willing to leave it there. Reaching for me with the quickness of a cat, he fastened his arms unyieldingly around me, his mouth, which was as pink and as soft as a woman's, moving wetly across my cheek.

Thoroughly repelled by his bold advances, I struggled quietly, pushing against him with all of my strength.

"Let me go! Do you understand?" I demanded beneath my breath. "You don't know what you're doing! Release me at once!"

He laughed softly, a viciously leering sound that filled me further with distaste. I did not want to alert the others unless I had to. I dreaded to think what Emma would say, should she come onto us struggling together in such a shameful manner. I knew instinctively that she would think the worst of me. While it was through no fault of my own that I found myself in such a distressing predicament.

In spite of the slightness of his build, there was a relentless strength hidden in Renny's slender body that surprised me, giving rise to a quiet desperation, as I continued to struggle against him.

"Please," I begged softly. "Do you want to wake Emma and the others? Think what she would say if she were to happen onto us. Don't you know how deeply this could hurt her?"

"Why should you concern yourself with my feelings?" a voice said scathingly above us. "It wasn't enough that you succeeded in winning Greg Gallagher over, was it, you trollop. You must have my husband, as well."

I turned to see Emma poised above us, her face a white blur against the deep shadows beyond the landing.

"*Dannazione*!" Renny spat the oath at her, sounding remarkably like a spoiled child, his fun ruined by the sudden appearance of an overly protective mother. "Can't you see that you are interfering? Go back to bed!" His voice rose unpleasantly, blurred by the slavering wetness of his lascivious mouth.

Moving swiftly away from him, I said to Emma, "It's not what you think. I was coming down the stair and . . . and I fell," aware that she was determined not to believe me, regardless of what excuses I might try to make. Nor would the truth suffice. She was prepared to see no wrong in Renny, that much I had already discovered concerning their strange marriage.

"You're no different from Loryea and the others," she was saying in her dull voice that, even in anger, was flatly unpleasant. "No different from any of them," she repeated, reaching to clutch possessively at Renny's arm. "Come along, Renny."

Without so much as a backward glance at me, he yielded to her command, going with her up the stairs like an obedient child and I thought crazily; What choice has a man who's been bought and paid for?

I needed the warm milk I had set out to find more desperately than ever, and finding my way into Gertie's kitchen, I took out a saucepan, filling it from the crock of fresh milk that Gertie kept in the icebox, which was considered a luxury in a town where the daily allotment of ice to the mines was nothing short of prodigious. Tim had remarked once, over dinner, that the men who labored at the lower levels, where the high temperatures rapidly dehydrated them, often consumed as much as ninety-five pounds of ice per day each.

Seated at Gertie's oilcloth-covered table, it was hard for me to believe that even now, as I waited for my milk to warm, men bent over their picks and shovels nearly a mile beneath me, bringing up the rich buckets of ore that had made millionaires of men like my father and Greg Gallagher.

The fire in the big range had been allowed to die down for the night, so that it seemed to take an interminable time for the cold milk to heat through. It was easy for me to imagine, as my tired thoughts darted back to the chilling events that had overtaken me inside the shaft house, that I was no longer alone in the big kitchen. A lamp burned feebly in a bracket beside the door that led into the narrow hallway that gave access to Gertie's room, its dim glow casting me in shadow so that my silhouette moved darkly across the wall behind me when I went to stir the milk, giving me the uneasy sensation of another presence that seemed to mock me, mimicking my every move.

Chiding myself for being fanciful, I quickly filled my cup and went with it to the table, determined not to be like Cleo, who had been afraid of her own shadow. But the sensation would not leave me, and swallowing the cup's contents as swiftly as I could, I went to the sink, running precious drops of water from the dwinding supply in the big tank that stood on a tall scaffold behind the carriage house, onto the smooth porcelain. Satisfied that the china gleamed as brightly as it had when I had taken it from the cupboard, I dried the cup on the teatowel that hung on a rod attached to one end of the big stove and put it back on its hook, my fingers trembling a little in my eagerness to return to the comparative safety of my bed.

The big house was filled with an uneasy silence that rustled softly around me, filled with a myriad small, furtive sounds, as if it strained as its chains to be free. I had a sensation of being weighted by that oddly oppressive quiet as I hurried back up the stair, pausing briefly on the landing to listen, then as I hurried on, scolding myself again for being foolish.

The upstairs hall was deserted, as I had hoped it would be, and after giving a last frightened look around, I slid quietly into my room, closing the door swiftly behind me.

Chapter TWENTY

She was there near the windows, no more than a shadow, gliding swiftly past the pale curtains, interrupting, for the barest instant, the faint glow of moonlight that filtered in through the delicate lace.

"Isabel?" I asked tremulously, thinking vaguely that I had been mistaken. The woman in black had not died in the mine after all. She still lived.

"I don't want to harm you," she whispered softly.

A fleeting memory darted teasingly through my mind, leaving me troubled. It seemed somehow important and I tried to capture it. But fear had driven it away and I said, "Then why must you try? Why?"

I took a tentative step toward the black shadows cast by the looming wardrobe that stood against the far wall. Then stopped to listen, in an effort to pinpoint her presence.

"What do you have to fear from me?" I asked softly.

"It's you who should be afraid." The whisper came from behind me now, and I whirled sharply to face her.

But she was no longer there.

In the next instant, I heard the door latch click softly into place and I knew then that she had eluded me, opening the door stealthily behind my back to slide quietly out into the hallway. Going to grasp the knob in icy fingers, I leaned to press my ear against the carved panels. That same uneasy silence that I had sensed earlier reached to envelop me, as if she were there waiting on the far side of the thick wood, poised to catch the sound of my own stealthy movements.

I stayed where I was, my breath stilled to a mere whisper, wondering whether or not I dared to accept her challenge.

"Loryea?" I finally said, calling softly through the heavy panels.

There was no reply, nor had I expected there to be, and I dared then to give the knob a sharp twist. My fingers met with no resistance and I pulled the door sharply inward, leaning to stare into the gray gloom of the dimly lighted corridor.

At first, I imagined that she had gone. Then, as I started to turn away, I saw a hesitant movement in the shadows at the far end of the hallway near the servants' stairwell, as if she had taken a wrong turn and was lost.

A startling thought occurred to me: Was it possible that it was Isabel who had been in my room? Did she walk in her sleep? Did that explain why Emma had first seen the woman in black inside my father's house, following my arrival?

I could not deny that my presence had produced a disturbing effect on my stepmother, in spite of her continued determination to afford me a courtesy which reflected what she liked to refer to as her "refinement." But was her dread of me such that it had caused her to become neurasthenic, giving rise in her to some underlying fear that caused her to rise from her bed while she still slept, to don her widow's weeds and veil and go roaming about the mansion's dismal hallways in a mysterious attempt to frighten me away, one that she herself was unaware of?

I shuddered at the bizarre thought, thinking that if there were a sleepwalker at large in the big house, it could just as well be Emma. The ghost's peculiar behavior suggested some hidden madness, for it suddenly occurred to me that her performances had lacked conformity. That was the memory that had teased at me earlier: The voice that had whispered to me inside the vault had not been the same voice that had flung hoarse accusations at me down the echoing mine shaft.

What did it mean? Were there two ghosts? Loryea Labree and her dead twin, Laura? Did they both stray from their graves at night to haunt the occupants of the two big houses?

Heart leaping, I moved quietly along the hallway, in the direction of that hidden shadow. This time, there was no mistaking the swift swirl of dark skirts, as whoever was there flung herself headlong down the steep stairwell, the whisper of her flying feet fading into the seething silence that reached to surround me.

Without stopping to consider the consequences, should that swiftly fleeting form whirl around to accost me, I flew after her, half-falling down the sharply sloping risers.

The woman in black paused briefly in the shadows of the carriage house before striking off up the colorless slope to enter the cemetery. I hesitated, recalling the chilling circumstances that had surrounded Loryea Labree's death, able, even in that half-light, to make out the heavy mourning veil that covered the ghost woman's head and face, falling to drape her narrow shoulders.

The veil billowed behind her like the fragile wings of some eerie bird of death as she made her way swiftly between the gray headstones that cast their own dark shadows across the sparse, moon-silvered foliage that grew between the scattered graves.

Following the faintly illuminated tracks that penetrated the field of looming markers, I went after her, watching her change directions to head directly for my father's tomb, and I thought: What is there in the vault that draws her? What is she trying to tell me?

A gusty breeze had risen, lifting her full black skirts, whipping them wildly around her flying legs, the dark veil over her head bannering wildly around her. When it threatened to fly free from its insecure moorings, she uttered a sharp little cry, her pale hands flying up to clutch at the filmy headpiece. Swerving sharply to avoid an ornately looming headstone, she went with a final, desperate lunge into the marble temple that guarded the tomb's entrance. I hurried after her.

But I was too late. Vaguely, I heard the soft clang of metal ringing against metal and I knew that, once again, she had eluded me.

I had no immediate desire to follow her inside and I turned away, the breeze whipping softly around me, rustling with an eerie little whistling sound through the tough shrubs and grasses that clawed at my skirt.

Compelled by an oddly mesmerizing sense of tragedy, I moved between the lonely markers that were scattered down the slope below the tomb, my eyes straining to make out the names carved into the pale marble. I knew then what I was looking for and I quickened my steps, reading the names swiftly in that colorless light that turned the world around me into a black-and-white etching that only added to the strange sense of unreality that had come over me.

Dane Smith. Susan Bigelow. The darkly etched names leaped up at me and I moved swiftly along, searching for the name Loryea. Loryea Labree. As if by seeing her grave for myself, I could somehow erase the memory of that darkly fleeting form that had vanished inside my father's tomb.

A pyramidal mound loomed ahead of me, casting its own dark pattern unevenly across the rough terrain. I circled around the moldering pile of earth and stones, my foot sliding on loose gravel. An open grave made a dark gash in the mountainside, directly in my path. Flinging out my hand, I clutched at a nearby thicket, clinging tightly to the prickly branches while I attempted to make my way past that black yawning pit.

Perhaps the billowing of her skirts made some sound that was set apart from the quiet rustling of the breeze-whipped grasses. Or perhaps it was instinct that made me suddenly aware of her presence behind me. Poised precariously at the edge of the open grave, I started to turn, vaguely glimpsing her upraised hand.

But I was too late. Before I could secure my balance, her arm swept out to send me plunging on a rivulet of loose earth and stones that gave way suddenly beneath my feet to carry me into that darkly yawning pit, the brittle branches that I still clutched in my icy fingers cracking loudly beneath the sudden impact of my weight.

Above me, someone laughed wickedly. *Madly*, I thought, staring up dizzily into formless features that were lost to me in shadow.

"Fancy you wanting to join me here among these cold stones," that same hoarse voice that had taunted me in the shaft house said mockingly. "They dug this grave for Lily Lewis, the girl from the row who drowned herself in the pond down by the mill. But never mind. It will have to do for you."

Without warning, a handful of earth pelted down on me, acrid billows of dust rising to cut off my breath.

Then, suddenly, it was as if the whole world were caving in on me and, cupping my palms over my nose and mouth, I curled like a cat in the cold depths of the grave, my body convulsing in a racking cough beneath that cruel deluge of sharply pelting clods.

Chapter TWENTY-ONE

From out of the depths of my memory, Cleo's voice said, "If a grave is dug the day before the dead is to be laid to rest, death come knocking again. Open grave at night mean someone else gonna die."

I lay quietly, imagining at first that I was back home in Savannah, safe in my own bed, the fluffy, goose-down coverlet all but smothering me.

I tried to thrust the puffy quilt aside. But my arms were pinned inexplicably to my sides.

Then I remembered where I was and a sudden panic filled me. Someone had buried me alive, which accounted for the oppressive weight that held me down, the sharp stones that had been mixed in the loose earth beside the grave biting painfully through my robe. I fought to free my hands, my fingers finding the dry twigs I had pulled in after me. Struggling beneath the heavy burden of earth, I thrust aside a dust-caked clump of roots and branches, managing at last to wriggle free of the compressing layer. Whoever had sought to bury me had pushed only a minimum of earth into the hole and it occurred to me then that it had been their intention to make it appear as if in the darkness I had stumbled onto the open pit, setting loose a small landslide that had carried me into the grave, the gravelly soil sifting down to smother me.

Kneeling at the bottom of the macabre pit, I hastily piled the loose dirt and twigs against one wall to form a precarious mound. Scrambling onto the spilling pile, I managed at last to claw my way out of the horrendous hole that was not nearly as deep as I had first imagined.

Ignoring the soreness in my body, I moved swiftly away between the looming headstones, to find myself standing, suddenly, before the doors of the vault, not quite certain how I came to be there. Belatedly, I remembered that the woman in black had vanished into the tomb. Then who was it that had come flying at me from behind to nudge me into the open grave? I found myself wondering. Who among them was mad?

The doors to the vault stood ajar. Pushing my way between the iron panels, I glided against cold stone to the place where I had left the lantern I had used that first time. Fumbling on the cold floor, I found a match that I had dropped and had not bothered to retrieve, stunned, as I had been, by the sound of Greg's voice calling me by a dead woman's name. Lifting the glass globe, I turned up the lantern's charred wick, and striking the match against the stone wall, held the sputtering flame to the narrow strip of oil-soaked fabric.

As had happened before, I felt drawn to the casket that held my father's remains, as if he was trying, in some mysterious way, to make his will known to me from beyond the grave. Thrusting the light before me, I went toward the window behind which he rested, the tiny tongue of fire reflecting eerily in the beveled pane.

This time, the answer I sought was swift in coming, rising up from the depths of my mind in that same uncanny way that I had known that I must call on his attorneys. Although my visit to Roy Gridley's office had proved to be fruitless, I was able to tell myself now that it had been a necessary step in a broader scheme of things that was slowly making itself known to me, as it suddenly occurred to me that the legacy my father had meant for me to have might very well be hidden inside the vault itself.

Filled with purpose, I moved quickly along the stone

walls, my fingers deftly exploring the seams between the heavy blocks. It would have been a simple matter for my father to slip up the slope to the vault, the night he had received the mysterious summons that had resulted in his death, to slide the document he had told me about in his letter into one of the empty crypts that awaited the remains of Isabel and the Steps. The smoothly dressed stones rested loosely in their places, ready to be lifted free when the time came to fill those empty spaces.

But search as I might, I failed to find the precious piece of paper or even any evidence that it might once have been there. Pressing my forehead against one of the glittering stones, I pounded my fist against the grainy surface, overcome by a fit of frustration and despair.

"You've come," a voice said softly from the depths of the vault.

I spun around, holding the lantern high. The woman in black stood near the rear of the huge tomb, her voluminous skirt and trailing veil etching a fearful, black shadow against the ashen stones.

Bracing my shaking knees, I said, "Is this what you wanted? For me to follow you here so that you could try to kill me again? Why? Why must you play these cruel tricks on me?"

"Not you," the shadowy woman said. "Not you. You shouldn't have come."

"Who were you looking for then? Which one of them were you after?" I asked in a strange, toneless voice.

"It's none of your concern." The soft voice, issuing from that faceless, dark form, sent a cold wave of terror through me when I recalled again the gruesome details of Loryea Labree's death. "Go away! Go away!"

"But I belong here," I said in quaking defiance. "In my father's house."

"Then go. Go back there and leave me in peace."

She seemed to fade, then, as had happened that other time, blending into the black shadows at the back of the vault until all that remained was a darkly yawning mouth that drew slowly closed, as if the mountain itself had opened to swallow her.

Was I mad? Hallucinating, perhaps, because of the spill I had taken into the open grave? I inched slowly forward, directing the beam from my light onto the stones at the rear of the vault, staring at that bleakly solid wall in frozen bewilderment. Who was she? Where had she disappeared to? I was convinced that she had been real. I had heard the soft swish of her black skirts when she had appeared in my room. And later, the hand that had flashed out to send me flying into the open grave had been quick and strong, leaving its burning imprint on my back.

Breaking free of the icy dread that held me paralyzed, I moved slowly along the rear wall of the tomb, running my fingers swiftly along the seams between the smoothly cut stones, thinking that there had to be hinges hidden there, to explain the ghost-woman's uncanny disappearances. My foot nudged against a ridge in the stone floor and a cold breath of air washed over me. I knew then that I had found the catch I sought and I knelt to feel for the hidden lever. Almost at once, the rear of the tomb began, slowly, to move, a section of the wall turning inward to reveal what appeared to be, at first glance, a bottomless pit.

Overcoming my initial sense of horror as I recalled that other plummeting shaft from which there had been no escape when the ghost-woman had sent me plunging to its bottom in the flimsy cage, I went by sheer force of will to look into that darkly yawning chasm. A narrow ladder hung at the edge of the dark opening and, as my eyes adjusted to the gloom beyond the circle of light cast by my lantern, I made out the gray-white shimmer of broken ore a dozen feet below me.

Like Alice walking through the looking glass, I started downward, the lantern swaying dangerously as I descended on the slippery rungs into that oddly beckoning chamber.

She was there waiting, her uncertain form barely discernible against the dark mouth of a tunnel that opened off of the main chamber. A framework of roughly hewn timbers framed the opening in which she stood, imbuing her ghostly presence with an oddly dimensional effect so that I had the uncanny sensation of peering into some forbidden netherworld through the black glass of a witch's mirror.

Then suddenly she was gone, fading abruptly into darkness and there was no one there at all. Numbly, I thought,

I am going mad. It was inconceivable to imagine that any human being could succeed in finding his or her way through the endless maze of shafts and tunnels without a light to illuminate the pitfalls. I shuddered to imagine what might happen to anyone who was foolhardy enough to try it, seeing her, in my mind's eye, groping her way blindly into the lower levels with their rivers of boiling water and poisonously seething gases. Was she inhuman, after all, capable of dealing with darkness and whatever dread pitfalls the mine had to offer? I could not mistake those pick-marked walls and heavy timbers. Evidently, my father had seen fit to utilize one of the abandoned shafts by turning it into a tomb. It was like him to be practical. But what purpose had the hidden door served while he had lived? Did the others know of its existence? Or had he constructed it in secret, to provide a safe hideaway for his own private reasons?

A second tunnel opened off of the rubble-strewn chamber, opposite the dark opening that had swallowed the ghost-woman, and I went curiously to shine my lantern into the dim reaches beyond its arched opening, thinking that my father had been at home beneath the earth. The suffocating darkness of the mines had held no terror for him. In which case, it seemed logical to assume that had he wanted to put something away for safekeeping, he would have turned first to the secret recesses beneath the mountain that had been as familiar to him as his own parlor. Isabel had spoken of his fascination with the mine, that had bordered on obsession, those times I had sat sewing with her and Emma in the verdant shadows of the gazebo. Among the Steps, Tim was the only one who had shared his fascination. Tim and Greg Gallagher. The three of them were familiar with every nook and cranny of the long shafts that had been driven deep into the heart of the mountain, Isabel had said. The thought served to disarm me and I took a faltering step forward, half-expecting the ghost-woman to reappear.

But there was no one there in the depths of the second tunnel that ended abruptly a dozen feet from me, a miner's pick and shovel, their handles shiny with use, leaning against the rough wall at the back. A candleholder, which served the miners as both tool and weapon, jutted from one of the thick timbers, a squat, yellow candle protruding from the metal loop at its tip.

I have no idea what prompted me to continue on to the back of that short passageway. Perhaps it was some darkly shifting movement of the shadows which moved beside me along the stone walls that had captivated my interest. Or it may have been instinct that drew me to further explore the passageway. In any case, had I not done so, I should never have discovered the second chamber that opened off of it beyond the thick timbers that served to support a streak of gravelly red earth that was sandwiched between layers of solid rock.

The small room I entered was equipped with a cot, and at first glance I imagined it to be another of the underground infirmaries Mr. Gridley had told me about.

Then, as the light from my lantern penetrated the gloom, I saw that the cot was covered with a pink brocaded spread. The same pattern of roses was splashed incongruously over the stone walls, the lengths of satin cloth attached to the rough stone with miners' candleholders that resembled spikes, the round loop that was designed to hold a light protruding from their thick end. Fat, white candles marched around the pink walls in stupendous ranks, thrusting out of the wrought-iron brackets, and a small, Persian rug woven in soft shades of pink and blue softened the uneven stones beneath my feet. A delicate slipper chair stood beside a low chest, completing the room's decor, which was grotesquely out of place in the depths of the earth and filled me with an uneasy feeling that none of it was real.

I think I knew, even before I went to explore the contents of the chest, that, as incredible as it seemed, the room had once belonged to Loryea Labree. There could be no doubt in my mind when I opened one of the drawers to find myself confronted by a stack of fliers that showed a comely young woman astride a white horse, clad quite scandalously in a short toga and shocking, pink tights.

Why? I wondered. Why had Loryea seen fit to appoint the hidden chamber in such a frumpishly exotic manner? The row of candles lining the walls suggested a theatrical setting. Yet there was something decidedly clandestine about the gloomy room that would not be erased by any amount of flaming illumination. Turning slowly, I scanned the airless chamber for some clue that might suggest to me why the dead woman had gone to such lengths in her attempt to make the room seem cozy and inviting.

"There had been rumors floating around town for some time that she had taken a secret lover, a man of some consequence whom she was meeting clandestinely," Royce had said that first night over dinner. And later, he had hinted strongly that the man involved had been Greg Gallagher.

Did that explain why Greg had imagined me to be Loryea that night in the vault? Had he turned to the glamorous actress for solace, following the death of her twin sister? Had the two of them then become lovers, meeting secretly in the underground chamber?

The light from my lantern reflected in a dull, silver object that had been thrust beneath the cot. Bending to lift an edge of the brocade spread, I discovered a small, silver-bound trunk. Prying at the lid of the small chest with nervous fingers, I found that it was locked.

Going back to the larger chest, I searched quickly through the drawers for a key, finding what I sought tucked beneath the stack of fliers. Putting down my lantern, I lifted the smaller chest onto the cheap frame-and-canvas bed, sliding the tiny, silver key into the ornate lock.

The fire of gemstones leaped up at me when I lifted the lid, the shimmering assortment of faceted jewels attesting to the daring actress' popularity. I could not help wondering, as I sorted through the accumulation of bracelets, necklaces and brooches, which of the brilliant stones had been lavished on her by Greg Gallagher.

Had my father, too, been mesmerized by her lush—and scandalously banal—charms? I could not help wondering as I held a glittering strand of emeralds against the lantern's bright globe. The fiery, green stones chilled my flesh, and I recalled something Aunt Hillary had once said to Melissa and me: "True gems maintain their coldness. They don't take on the temperature of a room, as do fakes. It would do well for both of you to remember that."

I had started to lay the brilliant strand back into the chest when I glimpsed something white beneath the tangled cluster of beads and chains, my heart leaping with excitement. Lifting the jewelry aside, I discovered a thin packet of letters bundled neatly together with a length of red ribbon. I stared in stunned amazement at the name penned in a lacy, feminine hand on the creamy paper: *Renny.*

Loryea and Renny secret lovers? I wondered numbly. Suddenly it did not seem at all inconceivable to me that Emma's noble-born husband should have become involved with the stunning actress, product that he was of an aristocracy riddled by a ruthless class consciousness and double values. Loryea would have been no more to him than a cunning plaything with which to amuse himself, in an effort to alleviate the childish boredom I had seen in him on those few occasions when his true character had asserted itself.

As for Loryea, what had she felt? Beset by a slight feeling of guilt, I untied the packet and, unfolding one of the crackling sheets, began to read:

My dearest Renny, the spidery script said. *I cannot forget how angry you were with me the last time we met here in our little rendezvous which bears such piteous evidence of my attempts to please you by providing the alluring atmosphere you crave. But, as you must surely know, it would be foolhardy for us to transfer our meetings elsewhere. He has come to feel that he has some superior claim to my spare hours away from the theater where, Renny dearest, I shine only for you in my role as the tragic Ophelia. Had I but known you first, I should never have given him any encouragement to begin with. You must understand, my dearest lover, that I have not encouraged his advances in any way since the two of us have been fortunate enough to find each other. Being yourself a person of worldly sophistication, you can well understand how my name has come to be linked with those of my many admirers. The public has a voracious hunger for gossip and there are those who delight in supplying it.*

Folding the missive with its sadly imploring message, into the bottom of the chest, I opened yet another of the letters, my gaze quickly scanning the closely penned page, the name "Laura" leaping up at me.

There are those who imagine me to be a replica of my

dead twin, in spirit as well as in my physical resemblance to that angel girl, Loryea had written. *Greg Gallagher is one of those. That's all his interest in me amounts to. Perhaps he blames himself for what has happened. As for myself, if I were to permit myself to cast blame for her tragic death, I should drift hopelessly into madness. I must continue to give him the benefit of the doubt for what has happened, absolving him in my heart of any shred of guilt. Otherwise, I should be destroyed by bitterness. There is no harridan who can surpass a bitter and vindictive woman bent on righting old wrongs. You are my guiding light, Renny, dearest, steering me safely through those stormy shoals.*

What did it mean? That Loryea had suspected Greg of some wrongdoing concerning the death of her twin sister? Had she been unable to contain her bitterness after all? Was that why, in the end, she herself had had to die?

The haunting questions drummed relentlessly through my numbed mind, and taking yet another letter from the packet, I searched its spidery lines for the answers that continued to elude me.

This time, it was Emma's name that leapt up to sear my consciousness.

As ironic as this may seem to you, under the circumstances, Renny dearest, I recall telling Emma long ago that one day I would become a serious actress, famous for my dramatic portrayals of all of the great roles, the letter said. *I swore to her then that I would one day be courted by the crowned heads of Europe. Now, it seems, my dreams have come true, considering your own noble birth, although I had no idea at the time that I should one day find myself being wooed by a crowned head who was in any way connected with poor, dear Emma.*

Long ago. . . . My gaze flew to scan the page a second time, in an effort to determine its meaning. Had Emma and Loryea known each other before the two of them had come to Virginia City? As impossible as it seemed, I was suddenly certain that something like that must have been the case and I fumbled swiftly through the remaining letters, rapidly scanning their contents for some clue that would serve to explain the dramatic boasts contained by that other letter.

I found what I was searching for near the bottom of the packet.

I was playing in the California mining camps when I first met Emma and the others, Loryea had written. *They were billed as sharpshooters. The miners had unsophisticated tastes in those first wild days of the gold rush. They actually applauded Emma's ability to shatter the glass balls Marcus tossed up for her, with a single ball from her rifle. She was not nearly so refined then as she is now. She appeared clad scandalously in a man's pants.*

Emma, clad scandalously in a man's pants? I thought wonderingly, seeing her in my mind's eye, plain in her dowdy dresses, her features prim beneath her unimaginative coiffure. I glanced again at the page that smelled faintly of some cloying perfume, a single word leaping up at me: *Sharpshooters.*

Suddenly, I was hearing again the loud snap of a whip flicking venomously above the sleek rumps of Greg's horses, sending them plunging toward me. The sound had reverberated around me like the sharp crack of a rifle. And later, I had seen blood on one of the horses, as if a bullet had grazed across the prancing beast's sleek rump.

Nor could I ignore the chilling premonition I had had that first day, of some forboding evil watching from the tower room of my father's mansion. Whose presence had I sensed that day? Who had waited behind those darkly glaring panes, rifle in hand as if it were his or her intention to shoot at rabbits? Who had taken deadly aim and fired, to send Greg's team flying ahead in sudden panic so that it had taken all of his strength, coupled with the sharp sting of his whip, to control them? Even so, he had not been able to stop them in time.

Or was I merely being fanciful because the pieces seemed suddenly to fit? If Greg's horses had succeeded in trampling me to death, I would have been marked off as the victim of yet another unfortunate accident. But I had not died. I had come to, to find Greg bending over me in the crowd. A half-formed memory teased at me, of a featureless face hovering in the midst of the rough miners who had crowded around me that day. The face had seemed vaguely familiar, as if, even then, I had sensed the presence of the ghost woman.

The fleeting memory made me uneasy and I brushed it aside, glancing furtively into the shadows, half-expecting to find her there watching me from behind the thin folds of the veil that served to disguise her.

Chapter TWENTY-TWO

During the next few days, Isabel took it upon herself to introduce me to the theater. Properly escorted by Royce, we went on one occasion to the Jenny Lind Theater, where she maintained a box equipped with chairs upholstered in red plush.

But I found Piper's Opera House, with its dress-circle, parquet, and gallery, more to my liking. The dramatic offerings appealed to my romantic sensitivities. Nor could I completely ignore the feeling of importance it gave me to be seated with the others in the box where my father had once sat with his family to watch the plays.

On this particular occasion, Isabel had brought me to see a production of *Hamlet,* staged by a repertory company that included Edwin Booth among its players. I was not surprised to see Greg, seated in his own box on the opposite side of the large theater that had been designed to accommodate more than a thousand people. I did not fail to notice, with a wanton sense of satisfaction, that he was alone in the plush box, his weathered features scowling in grim contemplation of the evening's offering, as if he were present only under duress.

Was he thinking about Loryea? I could not help wondering, pulling my gaze quickly away from his magnetic presence that both lured and repelled me, filling me with a dismaying ambivalence that left my wits addled.

But I had not pulled my eyes away from him quickly enough. He looked up and saw me watching him, our gazes locking for a spellbinding moment before I turned forcefully to Royce, saying the first thing that came into my mind.

"It was kind of you to think of bringing me here tonight. There were no funds to cover such frivolities back home in Savannah, following the war. And before that, Melissa and I were too young for Uncle Grant and Aunt Hillary to even consider taking us to see a play." My voice faded when I became aware of the cynical amusement that had brightened Royce's eyes.

I knew, even before my stepbrother spoke, that he had witnessed the impromptu little exchange between Greg Gallagher and myself.

He said, "The expression on your face, just then, was far from frivolous, Julie, darling. You seemed almost frightened, as a matter of fact, as if you had good reason to dread a meeting with our dour neighbor. That rogue, Gallagher, hasn't proved himself to be a nuisance, has he?"

"I've scarcely seen anything of him," I said.

"I had a distinct feeling just then that you might like to," Royce quipped, displaying that same perception that had so dismayed me the first time I had glimpsed that hidden side to his character.

I could not deny that I was attracted to Greg Gallagher in a way that puzzled me. Was it possible to be attracted to evil in a man? I found myself wondering. Was I to be one of those perverse women who found themselves drawn to the brutal side of a man's character? It would not bear thinking about and I pushed the dark thought aside to concentrate on the lively scene around me.

"I believe we will all fiind tonight's offering rather unique," Isabel said in her forcibly refined tones. "Edwin Booth has asked the stage manager for a practicable grave to lend authenticity to the fifth act."

Grave. A small shudder passed through me as I recalled my recent experience in the cemetery.

"Don't tell me we are to ascend en masse to some nearby graveyard for that particular scene," Royce said in his cynically bored way.

"Don't be preposterous," Isabel said. "The manager has arranged for a section of the stage to be cut away."

"It sounds a bit extreme," I commented.

"I pity the poor souls who are to play gravediggers

tonight," Royce said laughingly. "They'll be forced to shovel in earnest if Yorick's skull is to be handed up from a real pit. The ground under this building is as hard as a board."

Did I only imagine it, or had his voice held some sly connotation meant to strike fear into me? I imagined then that I caught an icy glimmer behind Royce's brilliant gaze, as he launched into a colorful description of a former production during which human bones that had once belonged to some hapless Indian had been tossed up with shovels full of loose earth, to lend authenticity to the macabre graveyard scene.

"In all my life, I have never heard of anything so tasteless," I said when he had ended his gruesome recitation.

It was perhaps fortunate that the play was announced then, drawing his attention away from me when the actors cast in the roles of officers strode onto the slanting stage, Bernardo's voice ringing out clearly, "Who's there?"

The play was perhaps half over when the fire bells clanged, their wildly pealing alarm interrupting Hamlet's entrance speech in the second scene of Act Three. Almost immediately, the audience began to panic and fear surged through me, as I remembered Mr. Gridley's description of the dreadful fires that erupted in the depths of the mines, wreaking their terrible destruction and taking lives for years to come.

Royce had risen from his seat, as had Isabel, the two of them attempting to hear what a man clad in the rough garb of a miner, who had forced his way through the crowd to spring onto the stage in the midst of the startled actors, was attempting to convey, his hands cupped at the sides of his open mouth.

" . . . a lodging house on A Street," his shouted words came sketchily to me above the noise of the crowd. ". . . spread to an adjoining building."

"But that's not nearly so serious as if it had broken out in one of the shafts," I said to Royce, when he turned to grasp my arm in fingers that trembled slightly.

"My God, Julie. You are an innocent," he said disbelievingly. "We've only just finished building the town back, following the last holocaust. The entire business section was lost, not to mention some of the better residences located down the hill from us. Come along. I want to get you and Mother safely back up the hill before the streets become impassable."

"Is it as serious as that?" I asked numbly, reaching behind me to grasp Isabel's plump fingers in my own, as men and women thrust past us, seemingly oblivious to any but their own safety.

"If a wind should happen to rise, the entire town could burn to the ground," Royce said, forcing his way ahead of us to create an opening in the moving mass of humanity.

The flames were plainly visible when we stepped outside, leaping above the tops of the buildings that lined the lower side of the street, driven by a gusty breeze that sent them curling toward the buildings to the east. Billows of flame-stained smoke painted the sky a ghastly shade of orange, casting a reddish light over the frantic scene.

Residents scurried in all directions, fear plainly written on their faces, the sound of shouting voices overridden by the frightened scream of horses. Buggies plunged recklessly by us, drivers apparently oblivious to our presence, as Royce guided us through the pressing throng. Briefly, I glimpsed Greg Gallagher's grim features in the midst of a small crowd that had gathered around him, the group moving en masse toward the vicinity of the fire. I realized, from the expression on his face, that he had taken charge and was issuing orders. Then he was gone, swallowed by the crowd.

There was Mr. Gridley, not seeming to recognize any of us, followed by a birdlike little woman whom I assumed to be his wife. We started up the hill, Royce staying close beside us, his arm brushing along my shoulders.

"There's no chance of getting the carriage out of the livery now," he said. "We'll have to walk. Thank God, the wind is easterly. Unless it chances to shift, the house will be safe enough."

"There's water left in the tank, but not much," Isabel said, beginning to pant in her heavy widow's weeds. She had tossed a long opera cloak fringed with ermine over her gown, the acrid smell of singeing fur hovering around her as the sparks that flew over our heads fell onto the soft ruff that framed her face.

From the corner of my eye, I saw a third building erupt

into flames with a sound like rolling thunder. I knew then how rapidly the fire could spread, nudged by the lusty breeze that swept down off of the mountain.

I said, "I don't see how they will ever stop it."

"They'll raze the buildings in its path and haul off the timbers if there's time," Royce said.

"They'll need you and the others," Isabel said. "I'll send Gertie back down the hill with you. The sisters will need extra help at the hospital. If necessary, Emma and I will go. And you, Julie. There are always the wounded to attend to when something like this happens. Everyone is expected to do his part. Sam can drive us down later, if it comes to that. We'll have the carriage, in the event. . . ." Her voice trailed off, leaving the thought that was in all of our minds unspoken, as the flames below grew in volume, the sparks from the tinder-dry buildings rising high above us to float like brilliant orange and red butterflies against the night-blue sky.

It was as if the whole town had gone insane, the street around us filled with the hoarse shouts of frightened people and stampeding horses. Above us, the two mansions were ablaze with light. Fight fire with fire, I thought incongruously, the crackling roar of the flames growing louder, carried upward by the shifting breeze. I felt the first pulsating waves of heat graze my cheeks, fear tightening my stomach. The mine, I thought. We could find safety in the mine, if it came to that.

It was not until we had arrived at the house, out of breath from the steep climb up the hill, that I realized the reason for the many burning lamps that flickered behind the mansion's narrow windows. We found Emma and the others flying wildly through the big rooms, gathering up valuables, carrying them to the ore wagon Tim used to haul supplies to his claim. Already, Tim and Renny had loaded Isabel's precious silver and a number of the paintings and statues she had brought back with her from abroad. Marcus was in the process of loading several of the lighter pieces of furniture when we arrived, while Emma struggled beneath a stack of leather-bound volumes that had been hand-tooled in Italy to her own specifications.

I was struck by the incongruity of the situation, even as it occurred to me that, should the fire spread up the hill to devour the two houses, the missing letter that I was almost certain Greg had taken from my reticule would be lost to me forever. There would be no hope then for me to prove my identity. I knew what I must do, and making certain that no one was watching me, I slipped into the dark shadows on the far side of the house to dart into the shelter of a nearby lilac bush.

The fire raged more fiercely than ever through the town below, illuminating the sky, casting its eerie red glow across the thickly spaced shrubs. Sliding between the softly rustling branches, I made my way as quickly as I could to the stone wall that separated the two houses, running down the terraced rocks to glide through the iron-spiked gate that had been set into the spear-tipped fence where Laura Labree had died, no doubt as a neighborly gesture at a time when those who lived in the two big houses had viewed each other more favorably.

Lights burned brightly behind the ground-floor windows of Greg's mansion and I wondered if, like Emma and the others, Bertha Foster and Greg's Chinese houseboy were swiftly stripping the rooms of their valuables. Then I saw the small yellow man running toward the carriage house at the rear of the house, carrying a large, white bundle. Bertha Foster scurried out of the shadows behind him, carrying a similar parcel, the two of them climbing quickly into a buggy that was harnessed and waiting.

Cowering into the dark shrubs that grew against the side of the big house, I waited for them to pass by me, guessing that, like Gertie, Bertha was on her way to the hospital, taking with her a supply of fresh linens.

The way was clear to me and, wasting no time, I went boldly around the house and in through the back door. Pausing briefly in a spotless kitchen that was almost an exact replica of Gertie's, with its huge wood range and oilcloth-covered table, I attempted to gain my bearings, wondering where I should begin. Where would Greg have been most likely to hide the letter I sought? In his own room, which I had already guessed was located in one of the second-floor wings? That seemed a logical enough place to begin, and going through a door on my right that took me into a large wainscoted dining room, I made my way to the central hall where a broad staircase wound upward into the dim reaches of the big house. Picking up my skirts, I raced up the carpeted risers to find myself in a long, dimly lighted corridor with doors opening off of it on either side.

Choosing the door nearest to me, I twisted the silver knob, throwing it wide to reveal massive rosewood furnishings. I knew even before I began rifling shamelessly through the drawers of an ornately carved commode that the room belonged to Greg. Flinging his belongings carelessly aside, I searched diligently, my fingers feeling for hidden springs or latches at the backs of the deep openings before I flew to a huge secretary that stood opposite the tall bed, flinging back its roll top to dig deeply into the numerous cubbyholes.

But it was no use. The letter I sought was not there, nor was there anything else that might have incriminated him.

It was then that I remembered the cupola at the top of the house and the stealthy lights I had seen burning behind its locked shutters on those occasions when Dr. Quinn had come riding up the hill. Without stopping to consider the consequences should Greg or one of the others return and find me, I ran into the hall, darting along it in search of a stairway that would take me into that forbidden part of the house that, according to Marcus, had been sealed off following Laura Labree's tragic death.

Chapter TWENTY-THREE

As in that other mansion, a servant's staircase wound steeply upward into black shadows at the far end of the hallway. Lifting from its bracket one of the lamps Bertha had left burning, I turned up the flame, holding it before me as I made my way slowly upward between walls that crowded close beside me.

A door barred my way when I reached the landing. But when I tried the knob, it swung freely inward and I thought again that Marcus had been wrong. The third floor of Greg Gallagher's house had not been sealed off after all, following that terrible accident that had resulted in Laura Labree's death. Or if it had, someone had since unsealed it.

A narrow corridor extended like a dark tunnel before me, the bare boards squeaking beneath my shoes when I stepped through the open doorway to follow it past closed doors that, I guessed, concealed small, cubicle-like rooms that must once have housed a full staff of servants. Evidently Greg had no further need for the extra services they had provided. That, or, like Isabel, he had fallen short of funds and could no longer afford to pay them their wages.

Halfway along the tight little corridor, I arrived at another flight of steps that led abruptly upward, sandwiched between dark walls. This, then, was the way up to the tightly shuttered cupola behind whose dark panes I had glimpsed those stealthy ribbons of light. Now that the way confronted me, I wondered belatedly if I had been wise to come, for I felt suddenly disturbed, as if I were treading on treacherous ground.

Nevertheless, I stepped onto the bottom riser, holding the lamp high to illuminate the dark space at the top of the narrow flight, the glimmering flame reflecting like a brightly watchful eye in the polished metal of a doorknob. I knew, when I saw that brilliantly gleaming brass glaring down at me like the evil eye of a pouncing cat, that the door above me had been well used, and I wondered, as I had so often done before, what stealthy purpose the small room that jutted up so abruptly from the mansion's steep roofline had come to serve. What forbidden rituals were carried out there behind the darkly shuttered windows on those nights when Thomas Quinn came riding up the hill, half-falling off his horse, to slip quietly inside the big house, remaining until all hours, as if he had every right to be there? What strange secret bound him to Greg Gallagher?

Compelled by a seething curiosity that overruled fear, yet filled at the same time with a gnawing apprehension that sent cold fingers creeping along my spine, I started to climb, holding my skirt high above the tops of my shoes with my free hand to keep from tripping on that sharp incline. I had the sudden sensation of being trapped. But, as had happened before, the door at the top of the narrow flight opened freely at my touch and I was able to overcome the sense of panic that had threatened to send me flying back the way I had come, out into the cool night, with its wildly dancing fires that had turned the sky a deathly shade of red.

Turning slowly, I surveyed the oddly shaped room, the light from my lamp filling it with a myriad threatening shadows. Then, as I saw that there was nothing there to fear, I was able to give a low little laugh, chiding myself as I had so often done before for being overly fanciful.

The room had been furnished to serve as a small private parlor. A delicately carved tête-à-tête sofa upholstered in pink brocade stood before the heavily draped windows that would, had the thick curtains been drawn back and the locked shutters flung open, look out over the town. Dainty slipper chairs flanked a marble-topped table that held a decorative lamp, its glass shade leaded in a delicate water-lily pattern, and a luxuriously piled rug bordered with roses covered the bare boards of the floor. A dainty, rococo davenport desk completed the room's furnishings, standing on carved legs against the drawn draperies, opposite the gracefully curved sofa.

I received an immediate impression of exotic femininity that made me feel vaguely uneasy. I remembered that Bertha Foster's room was located off the kitchen. And in any case, the cleverly appointed room in which I now stood was entirely at odds with the spare housekeeper's drab outward appearance.

As I crossed to the rococo desk, still carrying my light, I realized that it need not have been a member of Greg's household who had used the room. There had been Laura. Laura Labree. It was possible that he had furnished the room for her, the two of them turning to it for privacy, as the tête-à-tête sofa seemed to suggest. Had something like that been the case? Had the two of them slipped up the narrow stair to the cupola room to be alone together, undisturbed by the household's ordinary activities? Had they thrown open the drapes and flung back the stifling shutters to sit looking out across the town at the pale mountains on warm summer afternoons, just as Emma, Isabel, and I did from the benches inside the gazebo, chattering idly over our sewing, taking the breeze and enjoying the scenery? I saw that intimate little scene all too clearly, Greg seated on one half of the twisted sofa, facing a girl whom I visualized as being very much like the girl who had worn the tights in the fliers hidden in the chamber beneath my father's vault, his handsome face breaking into a white-toothed smile, his eyes growing brilliant as he sat opposite her, drinking in her beauty.

I turned sharply away from the intimate little scene that etched itself with such painful clarity in my mind's eye, going to the breakfront desk that opened to reveal small drawers and cubicles containing creamy sheafs of paper. I still could not imagine why a light should burn so secretively behind the locked shutters on those nights when Dr. Quinn rode up the hill, and opening one of the small drawers, I searched for a clue that would tell me the reason behind those stealthy visits.

The contents of the small desk were quite ordinary, with nothing there to suggest to me why those lights had glimmered around the rims of the closed shutters, and I moved toward the windows, drawing aside the thick curtains and lifting the small hook that secured the louvered shutters, inching them open to look out at the fire that had spread with lightning speed to devour yet another of the cheap frame buildings that lined the narrow street below. It was only a matter of minutes before the flame would leap across to the upper side, I thought, hastily closing the wooden panels. If I wanted to complete my search, I would have to hurry, since Isabel would be wondering where I had gone, especially if the fire threatened to spread up the hill toward the town's more expensive dwellings.

I turned around, trying to decide where I should look next. It was then that I heard it, the unmistakable click of a closing door on the floor directly below me. I stayed where I was, my feet frozen in their tracks, as I realized that I was no longer alone in the big house. Had Isabel or one of the others come to search for me? Was that who I had heard moving about below me? One of them opening doors and peering into rooms, wondering where I could possibly have disappeared to so suddenly?

Or was it Greg, back from the fire much sooner than I had anticipated? Fear tightened my stomach, my whole body growing taut as I poised to listen. For perhaps a minute, perhaps longer, there was silence, broken only by the distant shouts of the fire fighters. Then I heard a faint footfall. Someone was in the third-floor hallway. I had left ajar the door that opened into the cupola. Now, stepping as softly as I could, I went to close it, leaning breathlessly against the narrow panels to press my ear tightly against the cool wood.

A floorboard creaked. Another footstep, louder this time, followed by short, quick steps as whoever was there ran lightly down the stairs, the sounds growing faint, then fading away altogether into the distant reaches of the big house.

Whoever was there had gone. I waited a moment or two longer to make certain that whoever it was would not return. Then, heart pounding, I inched open the door and descended the narrow staircase, the lamp I carried flickering unsteadily in my hand.

With my back to the wall, I paused to listen again, but heard nothing except the far-off sounds of the crackling fire and the wild shouts of the men who battled that voraciously leaping blaze.

I decided then that it had been Bertha Foster I had heard, returning to the house for more supplies to take with her to the hospital. Sensing the desolate emptiness of this part of the house, which Marcus had claimed was shut off from the rest because of Laura Labree's death, I glided along the darkly papered wall, opening the first door I came to.

The room I entered was totally feminine, like the room above, the canopied bed that stood against the far wall, between tall windows swathed in pink, brocaded satin, shrouded in yards of pale lace. A marble-topped dressing table stood opposite it near the door, plush-covered jewelry caskets symetrically centered at either side of what I imagined at first was an oval-framed mirror.

I moved toward the dressing table, the glow from my lamp illuminating the pale features of a girl, staring out at me from the oval frame, and for a startled instant I fancied that it was my own likeness reflected there. Then I realized that it was not a mirror at all, but a lifelike painting that had been attached to the table's dark wood where a mirror had once been.

Still moving quietly, I went to stare in numbed fascination at the face in the painting, thinking that it was Laura. Or perhaps Loryea. Since they had been identical twins, I realized that it could be a picture of either of them and that only those who had known them intimately would know for certain which of them had actually posed for the painting.

The eyes peering out at me from the large canvas seemed oddly real and it was all I could do to tear my own gaze away from their lifelike stare. As I did so, I became suddenly aware of a subtle perfume clinging to the still air around me, teasing at my memory. In the next instant I recognized it as the same faintly musky scent that had clung to the pages of the letters I had found in the chamber beneath my father's tomb and that had been addressed to Renny.

A peculiar sensation went through me and, going to the wardrobe, I opened the heavily carved doors. Black cloaks and dresses hung like shrouds from the padded hangers.

"There's no mistaking those black rags she wears," Emma had said of Loryea. "And the veil. . . ."

At the back of the wardrobe, high up, was a narrow shelf with milliner's boxes rowed neatly along it. Standing on tiptoe, I brought down one of the boxes. I think I knew, even before I lifted the quilted lid, what I would find inside.

I gingerly touched the mourning veil, lifting the fine folds of black net, as if by doing so I could convince myself that the ghost-woman I had seen had been real after all, and not some frightening figment of my fancy. But who? Who was she if Loryea Labree was dead?

I had started to drop the veil back into the box when an edge of paper with bold words inscribed on it in a large, masculine-looking hand caught my eye. There were other papers folded into the bottom of the box, beneath the voluminous yards of fine net. Pulse pounding in my throat, I dropped the veil carelessly at my feet, and putting the box on the floor, I crouched over it, bold words leaping up at me as I unfolded the crackling sheet.

Dear Father stop arriving on afternoon stage stop your loving daughter stop Julie.

It was the wire I had sent to my father, informing him of my imminent arrival in Virginia City. Apparently, the message had been set down on whatever scrap of paper had been available when it came over the wire, to be delivered to him later. Who had been entrusted with the vitally important message? Who had failed to hand it over to Isabel, bringing it, instead, to this room that had obviously belonged to Loryea, while she lived? Greg?

Fumbling in the bottom of the box, I picked up an envelope, turning it over only to have my own name leap up at me. The letter was addressed to me at Uncle Grant's address in Savannah. I recognized the handwriting as Isabel's. This, then, was the letter she had sent me to inform me that my father was dead. Numbly, as I had done with the wire, I wondered who it had been entrusted to. Who had offered to post the letter for her? Then had brought it here to this secretive third-floor room, instead?

The missing letter that Melissa had kept hidden from me for nearly a year was there beneath the others, just as I had known it would be. The envelope was much bulkier than I remembered it and pulling back the flap, I saw that someone had folded yet another paper inside with the letter. Unfolding the heavy parchment, I saw that it was a legal document; a deed to a mining claim made out in my name. A second paper was folded in with the first, bearing my father's handwriting and a carefully sketched map.

This rich, undisclosed strike is to be yours, my dear daughter, he had written. *No one else knows about it. But I assure you, Julie, it is worth having. I have brought down several buckets of ore to determine the mineral content for myself, at the assay office. Tim found me at work there one night and assumed that the ore had come from the McKay-Ritchie. I let him and the others believe that, to protect your legacy. . . .*

Tim. And the others. They had used the ore from the undisclosed strike to salt the mine when Isabel had relented to Greg's persistent efforts to buy it, I thought. They had actually believed that the rich ore had come out of the McKay-Ritchie. But it had not come from there, at all. Who had known that? Greg? Was he determined to take my legacy from me, even if it meant killing me in order to make the strike legally his own? What if he should return to find me here? As quickly as I could, I folded the documents back into the envelope, and tucking the two letters and the wire into the bosom of my gown for safekeeping, I picked up the mourning veil and folded it carefully back into its box in an effort to cover my tracks.

I was lifting the box back onto the shelf when, behind me, the door opened. Pulse leaping into my throat, I spun around. The woman in black stood there, shrouded in a black veil identical to the one that I had folded into the box I still held guiltily in my hands.

She took a step toward me, the light from my lamp, which I had set on a corner of the dressing table, penetrating the veil's thin folds. Staring at her in horrified fascination, I saw that she had no face. Only her eyes were visible, glittering brightly out of a strangely shadowed oval that had neither nose nor mouth.

It was then that I screamed, dropping the box to the floor with an empty little thud, lunging past her to escape from that featureless stare that looked out piercingly from behind the black veil.

Chapter TWENTY-FOUR

She made no move to stop me and, plummeting past her through the door, I ran as swiftly as my long skirts would allow, down the narrow flights of steps and out into the cool night that resounded with the far-off shouts of the fire fighters, mingling with the crash of burning timbers and the ravenous roar of the flames.

My first thought was to hide the letters and the document that affirmed not only my identity, but my legacy. If one of them wanted me dead, it was to claim the rich strike for himself. If the deed and the sketchy little map my father had drawn for me were missing from their hiding place, he would not dare to destroy me until they were safe once again in his own hands.

He. I realized that I was thinking of Greg and, as if I

could escape from those darkly tormenting thoughts, I shot up the hill toward my father's grave.

Behind me, someone shouted my name. *Tim.* Ignoring his sharp summons, I continued on up the mountain toward the white pillars that marked the entrance to the vault.

Pausing briefly to catch my breath, I dared to glance down at the mansion. Marcus and Renny appeared, carrying a large trunk between them, its weight dragging at their shoulders. Isabel followed them out through the back door, a bundle containing some coveted object clutched tightly to her breast. Tim rushed forward to assist her, my harassed flight evidently forgotten as he took the bundle carefully from her to load it into the wagon.

Pulling my gaze away from that harried pantomime, I looked again at the fire that flared savagely against the velvet sky, billows of orange smoke rolling up like poisonous clouds. Even so, I could see that the fighters had made some progress in controlling the flames that were contained in the block where the fire had originated. For all of Isabel's frantic desire to salvage what she could from the big house, I doubted that the fire would come up the hill.

As I continued to climb, I turned around, pressing my hand to the bosom of my gown to make certain that the precious papers were still there, blending as quickly as I could into the dark shadows behind the marble colonnades that guarded the vault's doors.

A reddish glow from the fire below penetrated beneath the ornate cornice, casting strange patterns across the iron doors that stood slightly ajar. I would have to rely on that sketchy light to show me where to hide my treasures, for I had brought no lantern with me in my haste to escape from the glittering stare of that faceless wraith that had come onto me inside Greg's mansion. Pushing the doors all of the way back, I braced them open, as I had done before, using the large stones that still lay nearby.

I already knew where I would hide the letters and the document that was my legacy from my father, and I went with them to the crypt that contained my father's casket, prying at the thick, glass plate that had been used to seal the rectangular opening.

I did not hear her enter the vault behind me, or move over the stone floor. Later, it occurred to me that she had been there all of the time, waiting in black shadows for me to come.

Now, I heard her say, "So there you are."

Heart pounding, I turned to face her. It took a moment or two for me to find her in the thick gloom that flickered with faint, red lights from the fire that leaped beyond the flung-back doors. She wore black, as she had that other time when she had followed me to the mine, the soft folds of the veil falling to hide her face.

But this time, whether intentionally or not, she had forgotten to disguise her voice.

I said, "Emma. I had no idea you had gone to look for me."

"I had no choice," she said.

"Did Isabel send you?" I asked as calmly as I could.

"I saw you slip away into the garden. I guessed you would come here, eventually. I had only to wait for you."

"Well, you've found me," I said. "Let's go join the others. Isabel may need us to help. If the wind should rise suddenly."

"Do you imagine I'm going to let you get away this time?" she asked in a cold, calm way that I recognized now as the voice of madness. "You should have died in the mine, like Father. That would have been a fitting end for you, since you were so determined to make us believe you were his daughter."

Vague memories teased at me, of a pale face half-glimpsed in the midst of the crowd that had gathered around me when Greg's bolting team struck me to the ground. And later, Emma's voice saying, when I joined her and Isabel in the gazebo with my sewing, "I knew when I saw you riding beside Greg Gallagher in his phaeton that you had come here to take advantage of us."

But there had been no way Emma could have known who I was that day when Greg had driven me to the mansion, following the accident. Not unless she had been present when he had called me Julie. Julie McKay. And had seen the wire that I had sent to my father to tell him when I would arrive, I thought.

Suddenly, I knew without a doubt who that pale, ghost-like face in the crowd had belonged to. I had lain unconscious for several minutes before Greg could reach me through the swiftly gathering crowd. There had been ample time for Emma to fly down the hill from the mansion, after she had fired the shot that must have been meant for me, but that had grazed across the sleek rump of Greg's horse instead, to make certain that I would not live.

But I had.

"I would have been rid of you that first day, had it not been for Royce," she said, as if she had seen into my mind. "He had no business following me to the tower. He opened the door just as I took aim, and startled me."

And later, had taunted her, I thought, imagining that she had gone up to the tower room to spy on Renny. Or perhaps even to kill him, in a jealous rage.

"But why? Why should you have hated me so?" I asked. "Father was already dead. There was no possible way I could have stolen his affection from you, if that is what you feared."

"Not Father! Renny! I've seen the way he looks at you. And that night when I found you on the stairs together. . . . I knew then that I had to try again. And again, until, finally, I was rid of you. Just as I was forced to get rid of Father."

"It was you who lured him up to the mine that night, by telling him a fire had broken out on one of the lower levels," I said numbly.

"I had to have the riches from the new strikes," Emma said. "I couldn't let him give it all to you, someone I had never even met. Not that it would have made any difference if we had met. Renny's ardor for me started to cool as soon as the mine went dry. I did what I had to do. Renny belongs to me. I won't let you or anyone else stand in the way of that. Do you understand? He's all I have and you wanted to take him from me, just as she tried to do."

"She?" I inched cautiously through black shadows toward the open doorway.

"Loryea!" Emma spat the name at me. "It was Loryea who stole the deed and the letters from me. She wants what belongs to me, even in death."

"The woman in black?" I said. "But you are that woman, Emma. You! Wearing Isabel's black dresses and mourning veils."

"That's what I wanted you to believe," Emma said.

"That's why I've followed you. Pushed you into Lily Lewis' grave."

Unable to speak, I tried to make sense of what she had just told me. Surely there weren't two of them. Two women in black? And yet I had just left a woman wearing black behind me in Greg's house. Had there been time for Emma to make her way up the hill, to slip into the vault before me?

She went on, "I knew she was seeing Renny in secret, meeting him in some hidden trysting place. It was easy for me to lure her up to Greg's assay office, under the circumstances. I wanted it to appear that he was the one who had destroyed her. And so I left a note for her, signed with Renny's name. Then when she came, I flung the vitriol in her face. I wanted to watch her die. But there wasn't time. Greg came by the office unexpectedly that night. But I knew when they had the funeral that she was dead! Dead!"

"But her ghost still haunts you," I said, past the violent fluttering in the hollow of my throat. "And if you kill me, there will be two of us to haunt you for the rest of your life."

"She should have let well enough alone," Emma said. "She should never have sent you the letter Father wrote. I knew what she had done when the letter from you arrived. And then the wire, saying you were in California and would be coming in on the stage. . . ." Emma hesitated and I heard her gown rustling. Then saw the evil glint of metal flashing in her pale hand, reflecting the deathly red rays of the fire that still raged beyond the vault's open doors. "You should never have come," she said then in icy tones. "This time I won't miss."

My only chance was to dodge past her before she could click back the hammer of the evil-looking little pistol. An Alan's pepperbox, I thought. One of the wicked little guns adventuresome women carried in their reticules as a means of protecting themselves. Aunt Hillary had wanted to buy one for me when I'd started West. But I had refused.

"There is no possible way that you can get away with this," I said, trying to sound calmly assured. "You won't be able to cover your tracks by making it look like an accident, if you choose to shoot me."

"There's the mine," she said. "I know all about the secret door at the back of the vault. It will be easy for me to drag you there, afterward." She raised the small gun.

I made my move, darting swiftly toward the open doors. But before I could lunge through them, a dark form appeared, blocking my path. In that same instant, the gun in Emma's hand went off with a deafening roar. Something struck me solidly in the shoulder, giving rise to a searing pain that paralyzed my arm. Without quite realizing how I came to be there, I found myself lying on cold stones.

"You!" Emma's voice said shrilly.

Vaguely, I saw two of them now. Two women in black, half-hidden in black shadows. One of them reached to scratch a match against the rough stones, the tiny flame fluttering like a red eye against the blackness, then flaring brightly as she held it to the wick of the lantern that dangled from her other hand.

Tossing the match aside, she reached to fling back her veil. Emma uttered a little scream, her back pressed against the wall.

I was dreaming. I had to be. For the woman who had appeared to block my way and who advanced, now, toward Emma, the lantern held high, had no face. Where brow and nose and mouth should have been, there was a formless mass of twisted flesh out of which her eyes burned with a brightness that rivaled the red lights cast by the flames that flared beyond the vault's open doors.

"You!" Emma said again, her tone hoarsely disbelieving.

"It's time the score was settled," the second woman whispered through violently contorting ridges of flesh.

"But you're dead! Dead!" Emma lunged at her, arms wildly flailing.

The second woman—Loryea, I thought numbly—eluded her, stepping backward into the depths of the vault. The wall behind her opened and, as Emma plunged after her, swinging the little gun up in a threatening gesture, she stepped through the secret doorway, onto the ladder that led down to the hidden chamber.

Emma followed, the secret door swinging silently shut behind her.

I was alone in my father's tomb. I lay quietly, a strange sensation of peace descending on me.

Chapter TWENTY-FIVE

Strong arms cradled me and I gave a low moan, coming groggily to my senses. My shoulder ached abominably and there was something warm and sticky wetting my gown.

"Just lie quietly," Greg's voice said. "You've been hurt. But it's only a superficial wound. You're going to be all right. Tom has promised me that."

Tom. Dr. Thomas Quinn. Someone had shot at me but had hit one of the horses instead. Emma. It had been Emma, wearing one of Isabel's black dresses.

I opened my eyes, struggling to sit up. Greg pushed me gently back against the pillows, his eyes bright with sympathy. And something else. Something that made my heart leap.

Beside me Dr. Quinn was stirring a glass filled with a brownish-colored liquid. He handed the glass to Greg.

"Make her drink that," he said. "I have to do a little probing to make absolutely certain the wound is clean. It will help ease the pain."

Greg reached to cradle me in one arm, holding the glass to my lips. Lifting my good arm, I pushed it aside.

"The woman in black," I said. "Loryea. Emma has gone after her."

Dr. Quinn and Greg exchanged glances.

"We know," Greg said. "Now drink this. There will be all of the time in the world to sort it out later."

"Not if you make me go away," I said.

"You aren't going anywhere," he said. "Not now."

I drank, then, the amber-colored liquid, warming my throat, turning into a little ball of fire in my stomach and dissolving to race along my veins, making me sleepy.

"Tired," I murmured to Greg.

"Sleep," he said softly, bending to kiss me gently on the forehead.

I came awake to find him sitting beside me, sunlight blazing beyond him, through the open shutters. My father's mansion was visible beyond the undraped windows, rising proudly above the face of the mountain.

"Isabel," I whispered. "And the others. Do they know . . . ?"

"I think they always knew," he said. "But no one wanted to point fingers. It would have been too painful. It wasn't until Isabel suddenly realized that both of you were missing and Tim remembered seeing you dash by him in the direction of the vault, that they admitted to themselves that she could be dangerous.

It was Tim who found you. And who heard the second shot, in the old tunnel under the vault. Emma ran from him when he went down there. She plunged down one of the old shafts, before he could reach her."

"She's dead, isn't she," I said, my mind still cloudy. "The woman in black is dead."

He nodded solemnly.

"It was Emma all along," I said. "Wearing one of Isabel's dresses. Emma was the woman in black."

"There were two women in black," he said. "Loryea didn't die that night when Emma threw acid at her. She lived."

"But there was a funeral," I said numbly. "A casket. Royce told me that you chose it for her yourself. That you picked a color that would have been becoming."

"Loryea chose the color," Greg said. "But the casket was empty, at her own request. She wanted people to believe that she had died and was laid to rest beside Laura."

"I know about Laura." A cloud seemed to pass over me, dimming the brightness of the sunny room.

"Did Emma tell you how it happened?" He was leaning above me now, that same grim look I had seen on his face before making him seem hard and cruel.

"Marcus did," I finally said. "He told me that the two of you had argued and she fell."

"I wasn't the one who argued with her that night," he said. "I want you to know that. It was Emma. I had invited Laura to have supper with me here, after the theater. Emma must have been watching. Because suddenly there she was bursting in on us to accuse Laura of having an affair with Renny. She claimed she had seen the two of them together. It was more than Laura could bear, being accused like that, in front of me."

"So she ran," I said softly.

He nodded.

"Poor Loryea," I said. "She was the one who was meeting Renny. She must have blamed herself."

"She never stopped punishing herself," he said. "She had become more or less a recluse, even before Emma threw acid in her face and ruined her beauty, slipping off up the hill to sit beside Laura's grave, roaming about at all hours in her gloomy black dresses. I imagined it was Loryea who had killed your father. I saw someone there near the mine that night. A woman wearing black."

"So you tried to protect her," I said. "And all the time it was Emma."

"Tom and I both thought it was Loryea," he said. "Both of us tried to shelter her. Tom was in love with her. He had some idea that he could help her and that eventually the two of them would go away somewhere, to begin a new life together. But I think we both knew it could never be. Not after her face was destroyed. No amount of whiskey could blot out the reality of the situation, though God knows Tom tried."

"Will he be all right, now that she's . . . found peace at last?"

"In time," Greg said. "All of us will be, in time."

And because I believed him, I reached for his hand, feeling his strong fingers twine tightly around my own to bind us together.